A LA CARTE

A LA CARTE

TANITA S. DAVIS

Alfred A. Knopf
NEW YORK

THIS IS A BORZOI BOOK PUBLISHED BY ALFRED A. KNOPF

Copyright © 2008 by Tanita S. Davis

Published in the United States by Alfred A. Knopf, an imprint of Random House Children's Books, a division of Random House, Inc., New York.

Knopf, Borzoi Books, and the colophon are registered trademarks of Random House, Inc.

www.randomhouse.com/teens

Educators and librarians, for a variety of teaching tools, visit us at www.randomhouse.com/teachers

Library of Congress Cataloging-in-Publication Data
Davis, Tanita S.
A la carte / Tanita S. Davis. — 1st ed.
    p.   cm.
Summary: Lainey, a high school senior and aspiring celebrity chef, is forced to question her priorities after her best friend (and secret crush) runs away from home.
ISBN 978-0-375-84815-5 (trade) — ISBN 978-0-375-94815-2 (lib. bdg.)
[1. Cooks—Fiction. 2. African Americans—Fiction.] I. Title.
PZ7.D3174Aak 2008
[Fic]—dc22
2007049656

The text of this book is set in 11.5-point Meridien.

Printed in the United States of America
June 2008
10 9 8 7 6 5 4 3 2

First Edition

A LA CARTE

1

An empty plate hits the stainless steel deck in the kitchen of La Salle Rouge with a clatter.

"Order up!" somebody shouts from behind me, and the noise level in the kitchen climbs for a moment as sous-chefs and kitchen assistants step and turn in their quick-paced dance. Servers carrying plates to the dining room weave expertly in among the bussers wheeling trays of dirty dishes away. Along the prep counters, white-coated chefs bend to apply finishing touches to warm plates—a curl of deep green parsley, a swirl of roasted pepper coulis, a scattering of white peppercorns. La Salle Rouge has a reputation for excellent meals.

"Order up!"

"Let's move it, people!" Even though she's yelling at the top of her lungs, our executive chef, Pia Sambath, is in a good mood. I can tell, because none of the line cooks look like they're trying to hide in their collars. Some-times, when there's a major rush on, the yelling turns into screaming and an awful silent concentration. It's not a good time to be in the kitchen then.

"Order up, table six!"

A red-jacketed server with a pepper grinder under his left arm hustles past with two orders of a creamy soup in white bisque bowls, the steam rising from them making my mouth water. I watch him pass through the chaotic kitchen, imagining him gliding into the dining room, where the walls are a rich, deep red, the floor is old polished hardwood, and the lighting is subdued candlelight in silver sconces on the walls. Maybe the server slides the soup onto a table for two in front of the long, narrow windows that look out onto the courtyard fountains. Maybe he takes the bowls upstairs to the rooftop seating and offers pepper to a young couple who are there to get engaged. It's happened before. La Salle Rouge is just the type of restaurant where people go to propose or mark fiftieth anniversaries with fancy entrees and rich desserts.

From my stool in the back corner of the room, I watch clouds of steam rise to the high ceilings from the metal sinks under the window. Smoky fragrances from a heavy cast-iron grill sizzling on a gas range mingle with the pungent smell of garlic and onions and the deeper tones of coffee. The silvery crash of forks and knives hitting the heavy rubber sanitizer trays almost drowns out my mother's voice calling me over the cacophony.

"Lainey? Lai-ney! *Elaine Seifert!*"

Sighing, I look up to see my mother standing at the far end of the kitchen, wrapped in a huge apron and wrist-deep in some kind of dough. Her close-cropped black curls are covered by a toque blanche, the white chef's hat, and her deep brown skin shows a contrasting smudge of white flour on the cheek, just below her dimple.

"Homework?" My mother mouths the word exaggeratedly, eyebrows raised, and I roll my eyes. Frowning, she points with her chin to the side door that leads to the stairs. I roll my eyes again, mouthing, *Okay, okay,* not needing her to pantomime further what she wants me to do. I hate the thought of leaving the clattering nerve center of the restaurant to wrestle with my trigonometry homework in my mother's quiet office downstairs.

"Order!"

The bright lights and swirl of noise and motion are muffled as the kitchen door swings closed behind me.

It's hard to remember a time when the restaurant hasn't been the center of our lives. Mom used to be a copy editor and wrote food features for our local paper, the *Clarion,* and she met Pia when she did a write-up on the culinary school Pia attended. Pia thinks it was fate that Mom wanted to invest in a restaurant at the same time Pia wanted to buy the old bank building.

La Salle Rouge doesn't serve much in the way of "kid" food, since the menu doesn't cater to people my age on a cheap date, but I've loved everything about it from the first. I started experimenting with being a vegetarian when I turned fourteen, but Pia still found things to feed me and taught me to be creative with vegetables and tofu. I like to think I'm the best-fed vegetarian in the state of California.

Pia's been really good about teaching what she knows, and I decided early on that this is the work I want to do—get out of school and get into the kitchen for good. Mom and Pia have created a popular French-Asian-Californian fusion restaurant that has gotten great reviews from food critics. They took the best of each other's tastes—Mom's traditional Southern flavors and Pia's French training combined with her vegetable- and spice-savvy Cambodian tastes—and pulled off what one food critic called "stylized food with unique flavor combinations in an intimate setting."

Whatever that means.

Three years ago, when I started high school thirty pounds heavier than everyone in my class, Mom and I came up with a light menu for La Salle Rouge, and it's been such a popular idea that Mom lets me come up with tasty, low-calorie desserts, which is one of my favorite things to do. It hardly seems fair that I have to walk away from all of that just to do trigonometry, but my mom says I have to finish school before I concentrate on cooking. She says it's smarter to have a "backup plan," and she's made me apply to plenty of colleges and check out business majors just in case I ever want to do anything else with my life. I guess that makes sense if you're anybody other than me. When I turn eighteen, I already know what I'm going to do.

First, I'm going to buy a plane ticket to D.C. and go to Julia Child's kitchen at the Smithsonian and leave roses. They don't let you walk through it, but somewhere—I don't know where—I'm going to leave a bouquet and a little note for her. Julia Child is my patron saint. She's the queen of all reasons people can do anything they want in life. Saint Julia didn't start cooking until she was practically forty, and she went on to do TV shows and make cookbooks and be this huge part of culinary history. She never got too fancy, she never freaked out, and she was never afraid to try new things. I want to be just like her—except maybe get famous faster.

The second thing I'm going to do is buy myself a set of knives. Pia swears by this set of German steel knives she got when she graduated, but I've seen the TV chef

Kylie Kwong use a phenomenal-looking ceramic knife on her show on the Discovery Channel. Either way, knives are what the best chefs have of their very own.

The third thing I'm going to do, after I get back from Washington and get my knives, is . . . get discovered. Somehow. I know I'm going to have to pay my dues, but I'm so ready for my real life to start. It's not something I admit to a lot, but my real dream is to be a celebrity chef. Do you know how many African American female chefs there *aren't*? And how many vegetarian chefs have their own shows? The field is wide open for stardom. Every time I watch old episodes of Saint Julia, I imagine that I have my own cooking show. The way celebrity chefs do it now, I could also have a line of cooking gear, cookbooks, aprons, the works. People would know my name, ask for my autograph, and try my recipes. All I have to do is finish my trig homework and get back into the kitchen.

It's six-twenty when I leave our house next morning for my Vocal Jazz class. Mom sleeps in late, so I take breakfast to school. I pull on a hoodie, yank my ponytail through the back of my Redgrove Razorbacks cap, grab my bakery box, then jump down the stairs from our building to the sidewalk. It's freezing cold, but I actually like walking to school. It's better than waiting for the city bus, which comes late more often than not.

"Why would anyone want to take a class at six-fifty-five in the morning?" my mother groaned at the beginning of the semester when I started getting up in the pitch-dark to get to school.

"It's a privilege to be invited to join," I explained. Ms. Dunston's Vocal Jazz group at Redgrove High has won all kinds of awards and has traveled to Austria and South Carolina, and there's a rumor we're even going to the White House next summer. And even though it's a zero-period class, we take our time getting into things. Ms. Dunston lets us snack and listen to something from the blues and jazz greats like W. C. Handy or Sarah Vaughan to get our heads in the right place.

When I walk into the room this morning, the music on is the Count Basie Orchestra.

"Good morning, Elaine." Ms. Dunston smiles as I walk past her music stand.

"Hey, Laine. Whatcha got?" Syria, a bubbly junior in the alto section, looks up from her coffee and follows me eagerly toward the back table.

"Hi, Elaine. I got you a chai latte." Tracey,.a soprano in my section, sets down my cup next to me. "What did you make this time?"

"Thanks." I gesture toward the box. "Meyer lemon shortcake."

"Yum. Save some for me," Ms. Dunston calls from across the room.

"Laine, this is so good," Alma, another soprano, sighs as she bites into the shortcake. "You're an amazing cook."

"Hey, I brought almond scones." Christopher Haines, a tenor, sidles up, holding out a bag. "They're from Copperfield's."

"Anything left?" Bill, a bass, pushes up his glasses and peers over our shoulders.

Since Christopher actually holds the bag out to me, I take a scone, just to be polite. It's a little dry, hardly up to Saint Julia's standards, but it's almost passable.

Ms. Dunston comes for her piece of shortcake, and a few latecomers rush the table to be sure they get theirs. I grab a seat and sip my chai.

"Copperfield's scones aren't as good as yours, huh?" Christopher is watching me, perched on the edge of the table.

"I didn't say that." I feel defensive, embarrassed that Christopher read my mind.

"Well, I can just tell by tasting them," he says, and smiles shyly. "Yours are best."

I smile weakly, embarrassed, but Syria grins and pokes me with her elbow. "He's right. You've got the touch, Laine."

"Well, homemade is always better than—"

"Don't be modest, girl!" Tracey laughs. "We'll all brag for you. Yours are better, okay?"

"Thanks." I smile. "Maybe I'll make scones for Friday."

"Oh, good." Ben pokes me on the shoulder as he passes. "Make blueberry, okay?"

"No, make that dried-apricot chocolate-swirl thing you did one time," Alma insists, and the group erupts in good-natured argument until Ms. Dunston drains the last of her coffee and turns off the CD. Then it's time to do our breathing exercises and warm up for those tricky chord progressions in "Isn't She Lovely?" I stand with a little warm feeling in my stomach.

It's funny that I like being in a choir so much when I'm pretty much a loner the rest of the time, but I think the reason I do is that jazz choir is like its own little conversation—only better. The basses go back and forth with the altos, the tenors argue with the sopranos, and everyone sings the right thing so it's all in balance.

Ms. Dunston rolls a chord and then instructs the altos to hold a B-flat, and so we do, sitting on the edge of our seats, backs straight, our voices a perfect blend. Unlike actual conversations, where it's easy to embarrass your-self and everyone else, singing with my section means I'm kind of anonymous but still part of the group, hold-ing my own, singing my part.

Altos are like the salt in a dish—the sopranos are too bland without us—and the tenors are herbs that would try to overwhelm the piece without the solid meaty notes of the basses. I love being just a part of the mix—nothing that stands out but important enough to make things balance.

As always, hearing our voices as we finally get the piece right—all the elements of the song coming together—gives me a huge sense of accomplishment. I glance over at Alma as we hold the final note, and her eyes smile like mine must be doing. Tracey holds up her arms, and we all laugh—the vocal harmonic gives her goose bumps. Ms. Dunston beams at us, and I find myself smiling a little too as I walk out of class. Jazz choir is almost as good as making a soufflé—almost.

The problem with choir, though, is that it's over too soon. Before I'm ready, I'm back at my locker, getting ready to face physics. Ugh.

"What is Murphy's law? Does the worst thing that can happen always happen? What is Newton's first law of motion? Does an object in motion continue to be in motion all the time?" Mr. Wilcox bellows questions, and I slide down in my seat. Mr. Wilcox is about six foot six with a blond surfer cut, and he paces as he teaches. He's convinced that he can make physics fun and exciting, but he's *embarrassing*. He sort of leaps around the room and bellows at us to "Ask questions! Get involved!" For some reason, the more he wants us to be comfortable, the less comfortable I get.

Today we're doing a "will toast land jelly-side down?" experiment, which makes me groan silently even while everyone is cheering that we're doing something interesting. "Grab partners, people," Mr. Wilcox bellows, and there's a general scraping of chairs as people move around the room. The usual couples and friends pair off, and I find myself glancing toward Simeon Keller's seat before I can stop myself. *Stupid, Lainey.* Simeon Keller *used* to be my best friend, but he's not anymore. Anyway, he cuts this class all the time, and he isn't here, so I don't know why I'm looking.

"So . . . wanna do this?" The tall girl across the aisle, Cheryl Fisk, stretches out her legs and runs her fingers tiredly through her deep red hair.

"Sure."

I like Cheryl. Like me, she's kind of a loner, so we usually get pushed into being partners in this class. She actually went to middle school with me, but she's so quiet I hardly know anything more about her now than I did then.

Mr. Wilcox pulls another loaf of doughy white bread out of its red and blue polka-dotted bag and continues putting slices in his battered silver toaster. The smell of warmed bread fills the air, and my partner breathes it in. Her stomach rumbles. Cheryl ducks her head, digging into her pocket with an embarrassed expression.

"I'm starving." She blushes. "I skipped breakfast, but I have a granola bar in here somewhere. I swear I won't eat the experiment."

"You don't want to eat this stuff, I promise you," I reply as Mr. Wilcox slides a stack of paper towels, a plate of dry toast, a packet of jam, and a plastic knife onto our work space. The anemic toast slices make me shudder. "I mean, the name: should we really *wonder* about bread?"

Cheryl snorts. "Good point."

"People, be sure to put the paper towels where the toast will fall," calls Mr. Wilcox, moving around the room. "And before you drop the first slice, make a prediction. Is it going to land up? Is it going to land down?"

"Is it still good if it has a bite out of it?" someone yells back.

Involuntarily, I glance over my shoulder. For a moment, I thought that was Sim. He's funny in that kind of snarky, sarcastic way that drives teachers nuts, and I could see him eating his experiment just to get on Mr. Wilcox's nerves.

"Ready?" Cheryl asks through a mouthful of granola bar.

"As I'll ever be."

Cheryl pushes the toast, and it lands, unpredictably, on its back.

"Well, that was exciting," I sigh. "We're supposed to do this twenty times?"

"*And* write our *observations*," Cheryl reminds me perkily.

She carefully picks up the bread and nods to me. "Your turn."

"Great." I nudge the bread off the desk. It splats onto its face.

Cheryl is a good partner. She quietly does her half of the work, and I do mine. It is completely monotonous. No wonder Sim cut today.

Him again! I give the bread a particularly vicious jab. It flips off the edge of the desk and bounces.

"Oops."

"Think we get extra points if it flips twice?"

I have to stop thinking about Simeon.

I mean, he was my best friend. But that's *was*. Past tense. We met each other in grade school—when Simeon's older brother, Carrigan, got held back into our class. Carrigan tortured everybody smaller than him in our class, and when he came over to play once, he broke my Easy Bake Oven—*on purpose*. It was war from then on.

Carrigan was a jerk to everyone, but he treated Simeon worst of all—broke his glasses, stole his watch, broke the lock on his locker since he couldn't figure out the combination. If there was anyone picking on Sim, Carrigan was leading the charge. The day in sixth grade that Carrigan "accidentally" tripped Sim and made him cry during a game of capture the flag, I'd had enough. On behalf of all the other nerds at Redbud Middle School, I kicked Carrigan right where it counts and made a friend—and an enemy—for life. Everybody called me Simeon's girlfriend for the rest of the school year, but I didn't care. Nobody breaks my Easy-Bake Oven.

"Ten more to go," Cheryl cheers sarcastically, picking up the bread again. "Woo-hoo!"

"My observation is that this is the most boring assignment I've ever done," I say.

"Mr. Wilcox says our write-up should include any 'lingering questions' we have about this experiment. I have one: Why do I care?"

"That's pretty much the only question I have."

Another Sim-ism. I glance over at his desk before I can stop myself.

Sim Keller and I were pretty much inseparable right on through middle school. We used to hang out at the restaurant after school in sixth grade, when it was still new and exciting to me. Mom would give us a plate of cookies and sit us on stools, safely out of the way,' to watch the action. "And don't touch anything," she would instruct us. Most of the time, we didn't. Sim started calling the time we hung out together "kindergarten," because of the cookies and milk.

In eighth grade, when Mom decided I was trustworthy enough to go home after school instead of be at the restaurant, the tradition continued. Sim came over, and we had cookies—now cookies I baked—and did our homework while watching TV. Everything was fine, right until the time he brought Rachel Sconza over after school.

"So, you guys are here, by yourselves, every day?" Rachel's dark eyebrows were lifted.

"Well . . . yeah," I said, feeling my neck heat.

"So, is he a good kisser or what?" Rachel was the most popular girl in the eighth grade, and she'd already had two boyfriends.

"Uh . . ." I felt my neck scorch. "I . . . we . . ."

"You mean, you haven't even tried?"

I shrugged, tongue-tied. I'd nurtured a tiny crush on him forever, but . . . kiss him?

"I'll find out," Rachel announced, and she yelled into the living room, "Hey, Sim!"

Rachel Sconza rated all the boys in our yearbook, and Sim got a nine out of ten for kissing. By freshman year, things got even worse.

I ran into Sim at his locker one day after second period.

"Hey. How'd you do on the quiz?"

Sim grinned at me, shrugged. "Okay. I went to a party with Lana Enriquez this weekend, so I didn't actually get much studying done, but you know Wilcox—I'll ask for some extra credit, and it'll be all right. He's cool."

"Lana?" I frowned. "I thought you and Fay—"

"History." Sim grinned and bumped my shoulder with his.

"That was quick."

Simeon shrugged again, his eyes bright. "So, you going to this Halloween dance?"

I shifted my books. "Nah. Don't think so."

"Oh, come on, Laine! You never go anywhere."

"Are *you* going?"

"Yeah. You want to meet me there?"

"Okay." I'd been nonchalant, but deep down, I was thrilled. In spite of everything—all the new friends and the girlfriends—it looked like we were still the same good friends as always.

The Halloween dance turned out to be one of the best times I ever had at a school function, ever. Even though Sim wasn't even in costume and I was wearing a green dress and heels and *wings* (I told people I was the absinthe fairy from *Moulin Rouge*), it was amazing. When we got there, Sim talked the guys who were running the haunted house into letting us play with the projector for a while, and we put up some bizarre effects on the walls. The dance floor was so packed we could hardly move, but Sim grabbed my hand and started dancing with me, and suddenly we were surrounded by all these people— juniors and seniors and kids from our own year—waving and slapping Sim on the back. Most of them gave me a nod too, like maybe I was a little more interesting since I was with Sim Keller. That night I felt incredibly cool, and lucky.

By junior year, Sim and I didn't see each other much, and I realized that I'd somehow become a loner. It isn't like he was mean to me or anything, not on purpose, really, but we sort of moved in two different worlds—his had people in it, and mine had food. And every time I've seen him this year, Sim has always been in a crowd I don't know. He, of course, knows everybody—from jocks to artsy goths to preppies to skaters to stoners. This year he's been super-busy juggling all his friends. I feel like I got lost in the shuffle.

Last semester, when Sim started cutting physics, I saw him hanging out in the quad during lunch, kicking a Hacky Sack, and I told him he'd missed a quiz—just to be polite, not like I thought he'd care.

"Ooh." Simeon's reaction was to be goofy, smack himself on the forehead as if he'd forgotten about it. "Physics, huh? Guess I flunked," Sim cracked, and all the guys around him laughed.

I smiled a little, shifting my weight around, waiting for Sim to kick the sack to someone else and talk to me. I watched as he instead concentrated on the sack, catching it on the inside of his right foot, kicking it to the outside behind his back, and then catching it in his hands. He stopped and tossed the hair out of his eyes, barely winded from his freestyle exhibition. The guys he was with slapped his hands and congratulated him, and he finally turned to me.

"So . . . did you need something?" he asked, tossing the sack from hand to hand.

My face felt like it was on fire. "Um, no," I said, flustered. "See you." I went to hide in the bathroom until lunch was over, feeling like the biggest idiot at Redgrove. The worst thing was he'd said something to the guys when I left, and I heard them laughing . . . at me.

What was I thinking? That I was some kind of cool skater type he'd want to talk to around his guy friends? I promised myself that was the last time I'd talk to him at all, the last time I'd care if he showed up to class or not. And it was the last time. I've seen him around campus, and I haven't said a word. He goes his way, and I go mine.

The pathetic thing is, I don't think he's really noticed.

Okay, enough. This is the last time I think about Simeon Keller today. Right this minute, I am going to focus on Cheryl and this wonder-what-toxic-chemical-it's-made-of bread. I won't think about anything but what I'm supposed to be doing: this exciting assignment that Mr. Wilcox has so graciously set before us. Right.

"Seven to go. Should we put the number of little hairs in the jelly as part of our observation?"

"I think we should," Cheryl says seriously. "There's got to be some kind of line of scientific inquiry we can answer about what's on the floor of the physics classroom."

"I'm glad we have the first physics period of the day," I say. "Even with the paper towels, the floor is going to be nasty by sixth."

Eventually, Mr. Wilcox starts bellowing again, so it'd be easy to pull out a pen and take notes and stop thinking, except that I don't do either. Instead, I find myself doodling: "Simeon Michael Keller." I cross out the name and sigh.

My teachers tell me I'm goal-oriented. My grades tell me I've got a decent brain—when I make the effort. I'm smart—smart enough to know that Sim's not worth losing sleep over—but for some reason, he's still on my mind.

It's not just that he's cute—although he is really good-looking, with that kind of little-boy-lost/bad-boy look going for him with his black wardrobe, his funny-colored amber eyes, the thick, long lashes, and the collar-length dyed-black hair in his eyes. It's just that I knew the real Sim, once upon a time. I knew his freaky parents, his brother, his situation, and even if he pretends everything's cool now, I know it's not.

I sigh and pick up my pen. That was then, this is now. I'm putting Simeon Keller out of my mind this MINUTE. Permanently. This drama is all ancient history anyway. Simeon was my friend, and now he's not. Period. I'm not going to waste any more time worrying about him. Instead, I think about the crunchy, chewy artisan bread we have at the restaurant and how I should try and make a loaf this afternoon. I have to do something to cleanse my soul after this class with its pseudo-food and factory-made bread. Maybe tomorrow I'll bring some to Mr. Wilcox so he'll know what real bread is supposed to look like.

Nah. He'll probably make me do another experiment, and I can't stand wasting *real* food.

SUPER SIMPLE FRENCH BREAD

SERVINGS: 12

BAKE TIME: 20·25 MINUTES

1 PACKAGE ACTIVE DRY YEAST (ABOUT 1-½ TSP.)

1 C. WARM WATER (100°F TO 110°F)

3 C. ALL-PURPOSE FLOUR, DIVIDED
   (EXPERIMENT W/ WHOLE WHEAT PASTRY?)

1 tsp. KOSHER OR SEA SALT

2 tsp. YELLOW CORNMEAL (TOTALLY UNNECESSARY BUT PEOPLE LIKE IT)

1/4 C. WATER

DISSOLVE THE YEAST IN WARM WATER IN A LARGE BOWL, ACCORDING TO THE INSTRUCTIONS ON THE PACKET. LET IT BUBBLE FOR 5 MINUTES. ADD 2-½ CUPS OF FLOUR TO DRY MEASURING CUP, LEVELED WITH A KNIFE (DON'T PACK IT). ADD TO YEAST. WHEN THE FLOUR IS MIXED, ADD SALT. TURN THE DOUGH OUT ONTO A FLOURED SURFACE. MAKE SURE YOUR HANDS ARE CLEAN UNDER THE NAILS (!), KNEAD THE DOUGH UNTIL SMOOTH AND ELASTIC (ABOUT 10 MINUTES). REALLY PUMMEL IT, BECAUSE YOU CAN'T OVER-KNEAD BREAD BY HAND. ADD ENOUGH OF REMAINING FLOUR, 1 TBSP. AT A TIME, TO KEEP THE DOUGH FROM STICKING TO HANDS.

PLACE THE DOUGH IN A LARGE OILED BOWL. COVER WITH A CLEAN DISH TOWEL, AND LET IT RISE IN A WARM PLACE (85°), FREE FROM DRAFTS, 45 MINUTES OR UNTIL DOUBLED IN SIZE. (PRESS TWO FINGERS INTO THE DOUGH. IF THE DENT STAYS, THE DOUGH HAS RISEN ENOUGH) KNEAD THE DOUGH AGAIN FOR ANOTHER FIVE MINUTES; THEN COVER AND LET REST FOR 5. WITH A KNIFE, SPLIT THE DOUGH IN HALF, AND LEAVE THE OTHER HALF IN THE BOWL, UNDER THE TOWEL. ROLL EACH PORTION INTO A 16-INCH ROPE ON A FLOURED SURFACE. PLACE ROPES ON A LARGE BAKING SHEET SPRINKLED WITH CORNMEAL. (YOU CAN PUT PARCHMENT PAPER ON IT SO YOU DON'T HAVE TO WASH THE PAN LATER) COVER AND LET RISE 20 MINUTES OR UNTIL DOUBLED IN SIZE. UNCOVER DOUGH. CUT 3 SLITS IN TOP OF EACH LOAF TO ALLOW DOUGH TO RISE HIGHER. BAKE AT 450° FOR 20 MINUTES OR UNTIL THE LOAVES ARE GOLDEN BROWN AND SOUND HOLLOW WHEN THEY ARE TAPPED ON THE BOTTOM. REMOVE FROM PAN, AND COOL ON WIRE RACKS. CUT EACH BAGUETTE INTO 12 SLICES. TRY NOT TO EAT BOTH OF THEM!

**#** SAINT JULIA TRICK: THROW ABOUT ¼ CUP OF WATER ON THE FLOOR OF THE OVEN (AVOIDING HEATING ELEMENT) TO MAKE STEAM FOR A REALLY CRACKLY CRUST. PUT BREAD IN THE OVEN AND CLOSE THE DOOR QUICK SO YOU DON'T LOSE STEAM !

2

"Hi, honey, how was your day? Grab an apron, will you?"

"It was all right," I tell her, editing the news of an impending physics test from my response. "What do you need me to do?"

"Salad prep." My mother nods to the stainless steel counter and sink in the front of the room where stacks of boxes of vegetables wait. "We're short a line cook, so we promoted Octavio for the afternoon."

"Okay." Salad prep is pretty mind-numbing—wash vegetables, slice vegetables. I pick up a knife and glance down the counter. Ming and Gene are cleaning mushrooms and Roy, another kitchen assistant, is already working, quickly peeling and slicing a white root. The sharp smell of ginger hits me.

"That smells good," I say, and Roy nods, glancing up.

"Clears my head," he says, and smiles.

I watch Roy's technique before starting in. The Japanese turnips slice into thin pale oblongs, releasing a pungent odor.

Mom slides a box of pale-skinned, round jicama roots toward me. "I need these peeled," she says, moving around me carefully. "Those turnips look good, but watch the thickness, huh?"

"Mom," I sigh. "I am not going to cut myself."

"I know, but you don't need to go that thin."

I roll my eyes. "Okay, okay."

Roy finishes with the ginger and reaches for one of the jicamas. I pick up the pace. His knife is quick as he chops the heavy white root, then matchsticks it for artistic presentation.

"Hey, Roy, can you cut that in slow motion?" I beg. "I want to see how you do it."

Roy glances over at me and grins, his gold tooth flashing in his smile. "Okay. Slice it in half"—the knife *thunk*s as the blade bites into the crisp flesh—"and put the cut side down."

"Got it."

"In half again" (*thunk*) "and start making slices, maybe a quarter inch thick. A jicama this size, you get eight slices; some are smaller, some are bigger. Cut each slice into four sticks. When you julienne, you don't want any longer than two inches, okay?"

"Got it," I say, concentrating. My jicama gives me ten

slices, and my matchsticks are skinnier than Roy's, but by the time I meticulously finish one, he's done three. I growl a little, glancing at his pile.

"You have the skills," he says. "Now you need the speed."

My mother glares at him. "Don't encourage her," she warns. "Don't worry about speed, Laine. It took me years to learn my knife work."

"But I'm not you," I mutter under my breath.

Roy laughs.

The noise this afternoon isn't as urgent yet as it is during dinner service. So far it's laughter, conversation, the rhythmic *thunk, thunk, thunk* of heavy knives slicing through vegetables and bone to make stock for the gravies and sauces, and the clink of glasses coming out of the sanitizer. The back door opens.

"Afternoon, everybody. How's my Laine?"

"Hey, Miss Maeva." People in the kitchen greet the stout older woman.

Maeva shrugs out of her jacket and pushes her red-tinted hair into a net before putting on her apron. The restaurant sends out all of the linens to a dry cleaner, but Maeva takes over the ironing, setting up with a padded board on the back counter.

"How's school?" Maeva calls, like she always does. The iron hisses, and the smell of hot cotton adds a layer of scent to the warm room.

"Okay," I say, sliding a pile of jicama peelings into a plastic bin.

"What's 'okay'?" Maeva scolds. "You kids! Can't you say something when somebody talks to you?" Maeva picks up a flattened napkin and folds it into the origami swan shape that Pia likes.

"It was . . . school," I laugh. "I don't know what to say. It wasn't here, that's all."

It's hard to know what to say. When I'm in the kitchen, everything fades: my bruised ego at Mrs. Stowers's surprise trigonometry quiz, my irritation at getting rained on without my umbrella, my cruddy physics lab, everything. The window in the kitchen is fogged with steam, and I'm damp and sticky, but I'm perfectly at home.

"It was a pretty good day," I admit finally. "Nobody died."

Laughter overwhelms Maeva's disgusted sigh. Even Ming, our quietest kitchen assistant, who's usually plugged in to her music, looks up and laughs.

Conversation continues around me, but I am struck with inspiration. As soon as the bulk of the salad prep is finished, I escape to a quiet corner with a piece of fresh ginger root and grate it. Last month's *Gourmet* had a recipe for pear gingerbread, and Mom lets me experiment with desserts when there's time.

Our pastry chef at La Salle Rouge is this big, mellow

man named Stefan Schlatt. He looks like a blue-eyed, graying bear, but he's always been nice to me. He has his bakers leave me my little space in the pastry station, stocked with flour and sugar and everything I might need. Mom makes a big deal out of making me keep the pastry station clean and thank the pastry staff every single time I'm in there, because, as she always says, the kitchen is not a playground. I know it's a privilege to experiment in here, and so does Mom, who sometimes does it herself.

I'm halfway through sifting my dry ingredients when Mom comes over and puts an arm around me.

"Looks good, Laineybelle. You using the Barbados molasses?"

"Yep. And I'm thinking of adding crystallized ginger too. And some black pepper. What do you think?"

Mom smiles. "I think that your gingerbread is not going to be for the faint of heart."

"Real gingerbread usually isn't."

"I see!" My mother arches her eyebrow and laughs.

"Did the mail come yet?" I ask quickly before she wanders away again. "Did I get anything from that bakeware contest?"

"I haven't been home this afternoon," Mom says. "Unless you told them you lived here, I don't know."

"I do live here," I joke. "My landlord just needs to put in a shower."

I check on my gingerbread and frown, looking around the pastry station for help. I spot Stefan and wait until he sees me.

"What is it today?" he asks, peering into my oven.

"Gingerbread. Is the top dry enough?" One of the things I always do to myself is second-guess when things are done. Even if I have a timer go off, do the toothpick test, and have Mom say it looks done, I'm never sure. You wouldn't believe how many things I eat that are just barely burnt, but sometimes that improves the flavor. Only sometimes, though.

Stefan pulls the pan out of the oven and frowns at it, gently pressing his fingertips into the top of the dark cake. "Did you test the temperature?"

"No . . ." I press my fingers against the cake. It springs back.

"Test it. Temperature inside should be between 190 and 195 degrees."

Stefan points me toward the probe thermometer that is magnetically attached to the front of the oven. I slide the metal into the center, being careful not to touch the pan. It is 193 degrees. I guess it's done enough.

The smell of gingerbread is the smell of a thousand afternoons with MaDea, the smell of wet sidewalks and lemon tea and all the things I love best about the end of the year. It's always so amazing to me that I can re-create

29

a time just through smell. I lean my face into the pan and breathe in deep. Yum.

"You know, most people would use a knife, but it might be fun to watch if you're going to eat that face-first."

I jerk back from the pan and turn around.

"S-Sim!" The word sputters from my surprised mouth.

"The one and only," Sim says, grinning. He's leaning against the counter behind me, wearing a black sweater over a white tee and jeans. His hair is messy, like he's been wearing a hat or out in the wind. I notice he has keys in his hand. Where has he come from? Where is he going?

Why do I care?

I shut my mouth and hastily pull off my oven mitts, trying to pretend a calm I don't feel. "Do you need something?" I ask in a halfway normal voice.

"Do I need to have a reason to drop by?" Sim counters. He's smiling at me like he knows something I don't.

I make my voice cool, remembering his blank-faced *Did you need something?* "Yes, Sim, actually, you do have to have a reason to drop by. This is a restaurant, and we're not open for dinner yet, so what do you want?"

"Well, look who's here!"

Oh no. Mom rushes over, her eyes bright.

"Hello, Simeon! What are you up to?"

Mom beams at both of us, approval in every line of her body.

"Hi, Mrs. Seifert." Simeon smiles as if my mother is his favorite person in the world. "I just came by to see if Laine has notes for our physics test I can borrow."

"Oh, right," I mutter. Simeon, even without bothering to come to class, is miles better at physics than I am, and he knows it. He could pass a test in his sleep, practically.

"No, really, Laine." Sim turns to me. "Wilcox is making me turn in notes 'cause I've been . . . uh, out sick and missed so many classes. So, if I could copy your notes . . ."

"I need them for the test," I say quickly.

"Lainey, why don't you guys go down to the office? He can copy them on the machine, and then you'll both have them when you need them."

I look at my mother and sigh. Could she be more helpful?

"Okay," I say grudgingly. "But I've got to de-pan my gingerbread first."

"*Elaine.*" My mother frowns in exasperation. "I'll bring you a piece. Go help Sim now. Shoo." Mom waves her hands as if I'm a balky three-year-old who won't go outside to play.

My mom wishes I had friends; can you tell? Anytime

I have a project with someone, Mom wants to make sure to send them home with cookies. Every time I go to my physics tutorial before a test, my mother says, "You could invite people to study over here. I'd make popcorn balls," as if this is all everyone wants out of life. I'm pretty sure she'd suggest a taffy pull if she thought I'd go for it.

(Actually, we've made taffy before. Don't laugh; it was really good.)

Sighing, I untie my apron and yank it over my head. I feel naked without it, and I feel nervous that Sim's here, trailing quietly behind me down the stairs. I take the stairs quickly, practically running.

"Hey." He grabs my arm, and I stop moving, my hand on the knob. "Hey."

"What?" I ask. I take a deep breath and turn back toward the door. He's standing too close to me.

"You just seem . . . mad. What's up, Lainey?"

What's up, he says. Please. Am I the only one who remembers that he hasn't acted like I exist since last summer?

"Hey." Sim's fingers loosen their hold on my arm and slide across my hand. He tugs on my thumb. "Can we just talk for a minute?" he asks plaintively. "I didn't just come to get your notes, you know. I thought we could, I don't know, talk a minute or something."

I pull my hand away from his, surprised and fumble-fingered as I open the door. *Calm. Calm. Calm.*

"What do you want, Sim? Really? You could've gotten these notes from at least fifty other people in our class."

Sim smiles a little, and his yellowy amber eyes crinkle behind their long lashes. "I know other people had the notes," he says, "but no one else had the *gingerbread.*"

Just give him the notes, Lainey.

"You know that was a joke, right?" Sim ducks his head to look into my face. "Laine, I know I haven't been around lately, but I appreciate you coming through for me. I owe you one, okay?"

"Sure, Sim. Whatever." The scanner is on the second page. Almost done.

"Laine." Simeon leans across the desk and taps my arm. "Look. How about if—"

"I've got gingerbread," Mom calls, pushing open the office door, carrying dessert plates. Simeon turns toward her, and I breathe out a quick sigh, half relieved, half something else. Disappointed?

No. It's not disappointment. I have way better things to do than talk to Simeon Keller. Way better things.

MA DEA'S GINGERBREAD
(LOW FAT VERSION 1)

SERVINGS : 8

COOK TIME : 35 MINUTES

1/2 TSP. SALT

1-1/2 TSP. GROUND CINNAMON (ADD CARDAMOM SOMETIMES?)

2 TBSP. GROUND GINGER

1/4 TSP. GROUND CLOVES

1 1/2 TSP. POWDERED MUSTARD

1/2 TSP. BLACK PEPPER

1/2 TSP. WHITE PEPPER (TRY CAYENNE MAYBE?)

1/4 C. CHOPPED CRYSTALLIZED GINGER (ADD ABOUT SAME
    OF FRESH PLANE-GRATED GINGER- YUM!)

1/4 POUND (1 STICK) UNSALTED BUTTER (4 TBSP. CANOLA
    OIL, 3 TBSP. PLAIN YOGURT - CUT FAT, ADD MOISTURE)

3/4 C. LIGHT BROWN SUGAR (TRY 1/2, OR SUGAR SUBSTITUTE
                         - OR MAPLE SUGAR?)

2 LARGE EGGS, AT ROOM TEMPERATURE

2/3 C. MOLASSES

2 1/2 C ALL-PURPOSE FLOUR
    (TRY USING SPELT FLOUR FOR MORE FIBER?)

2 TSP. BAKING SODA (TRY ONE POWDER, ONE SODA TO
    CUT WEIRD METALLIC SODA FLAVOR)

1 C. BOILING WATER

PREHEAT THE OVEN TO 350° F.

MIX FIRST 8 INGREDIENTS. ADD BUTTER AND BROWN SUGAR AND MIX WELL. SCRAPE DOWN THE BOWL AND ADD THE EGGS, ONE AT A TIME, MIXING WELL AFTER EACH ADDITION. ADD THE MOLASSES, AND KEEP STIRRING UNTIL A DECENT DOUGH FORMS.

THOROUGHLY COMBINE FLOUR AND BAKING SODA IN A SMALL BOWL. NEXT, ADD HALF THE FLOUR MIXTURE TO THE MOLASSES SPICE MIXTURE AND STIR WELL. AFTER THAT, ADD HALF OF THE BOILING WATER TO THE REMAINING FLOUR MIX AND STIR, THEN ADD THAT TO THE LARGER BOWL. FINALLY, ADD THE LAST OF THE BOILING WATER TO THE MIX AND STIR WELL INTO A LOOSE BATTER.

BAKE UNTIL THE TOP IS DRY, SHINY, AND SPRINGS BACK TO THE TOUCH, ABOUT 25 TO 35 MINUTES. COVER AND STORE AT ROOM TEMPERATURE UP TO 2 DAYS.

＊＊ MOIST, SPICY - GOOD. SEE IF MOM CAN TELL IT'S LOW FAT.

3

The best things about the weekend are

No physics

No trigonometry

No physics or trigonometry

It's pouring—again—and a nasty little wind is ripping all the blossoms off the trees on our street. As I gloomily slog through puddles, fighting to keep my grip on my umbrella, I'm feeling sorry for myself. *Other* people have mothers who make them soup. *Other* people have mothers who are home when they're not feeling good. *Other* people live in states where spring doesn't randomly decide to revert back to winter.

I pull up my collar as I step under the awning in front of Smith's Pharmacy. A gust of warm air from the front door convinces me I need to go inside. I have to at least buy a packet of tissues, maybe a cooking magazine or something. But just as I pull open the door, I remember why I never stop by Smith's after school.

"Elaine!"

Oh, crap. I let the door fall closed and turn around reluctantly. "Hi, Christopher."

"How are ya?" Wrapped in a green apron from Smith's Pharmacy, Christopher Haines stands on the sidewalk, his arms crossed and his hands tucked under his arms. Anyone can see that he's cold, even in his gray sweater. Anyone with sense would have at least put a coat on before going outside. Of course, Chris Haines has no sense.

"I'm fine." My voice sounds like lead, even to me.

"So . . ." Christopher shifts, biting his bottom lip nervously. "I haven't seen you much outside of Vocal Jazz."

That's because I've seen you first. "I've been busy," I say lamely.

"Oh." The conversation dies. How long am I going to be trapped here in the wet because Christopher Haines is an idiot?

I shouldn't be so mean. Christopher is the son of one of Mom's best friends. Our families used to hang out when we were in grade school, both of us missing teeth and singing our hearts out in the middle school chorus. Back then, Christopher used to be plain old Chris: short, tan-skinned, dark curly-haired, and nerdy—pretty average like the rest of the boys in our class. He was okay—even Sim said he was a good kid, since he never tattled when Sim teased him. But somewhere between our sophomore and junior year, his family went to Europe or something, and he turned into someone else—someone tall, okay-looking, better-dressed, with bleached dreads, with less acne, and without a mouthful of braces. Someone who changed his name to Topher.

"So, what are you doing?"

"Standing in front of the store?"

Christopher ducks his head, his light brown skin flushing. "Dumb question, huh?"

"Actually, I think I'll just go home," I say, and open my umbrella. "I think I have a cold coming on."

"We have chicken soup," Christopher says immediately. "Oh, wait, you're vegetarian. But we have cold medicine. Aisle five."

"Thanks, Christopher, but . . . no. I'm just going home."

"I hope you feel better," Christopher says dutifully.

"Yep. See you, Chris."

"Um, Elaine?"

Sighing, I half turn. The wind is slanting the rain down at an angle, and Christopher is getting wet. I shift so my umbrella is blocking the rain from the back of my neck. "What?"

"Do you . . . Are you ever going to call me Topher?"

I shrug wearily. "Maybe. Maybe not. Bye."

I know I shouldn't mess with him. He's just too easy.

I push off my hood, running my fingers through my damply snarled hair as I walk up the stairs to our front door. In the mailbox, I see an envelope from *Southern Cooking* and rip the thin letter open quickly.

Congratulations, blah blah blah, *honorable mention,* blah blah blah, *subscription to our magazine,* blah blah.

Honorable mention. Not bad, since the category I entered was for a main course using turkey, and I've never cooked a whole turkey in my life. I wish I'd won money, since I'm still saving up for my pilgrimage to Saint Julia's at the Smithsonian, but a free magazine is okay too.

I change into sweats and restlessly poke through the fridge, trying to find something I'm in the mood to eat. The phone rings, and the clattering noises in the background let me know who it is even without checking caller ID.

"Hey, Mom."

"Hey, Laineybelle. Not coming down for dinner?"

"Nope . . . I'm pretty tired. My throat is scratchy, and I just want to go to bed and watch a movie."

"I wish I could," Mom says enviously. "With all this rain, it'll probably be a pretty quiet night, though. Maybe I'll get home early."

"That would be nice. I was just wishing *someone* would make me some soup."

"*Someone* would make you some if she could. Did you find the garlic in the broiler?"

"Garlic?"

"I baked a few cloves last night for salad dressing, remember? You could use some of them and make some garlic mashed potatoes. Garlic's good for a cold."

"Mom, *potatoes*. Please. Just because I'm sick, I'm not going to load up on carbs."

"Oh, you and your carbohydrates," my mother says with disgust. "Well, don't just sit around all night drinking tea and feeling sorry for yourself. Eat something decent, all right?"

Feeling sorry for myself? "I'm going to make some garlic roasted beets."

"Ooh, that sounds good. There's leftover pasta in the fridge."

"I know."

Mom's voice softens. "Well, have a good evening, honey. I'm sorry I can't get away to make you something myself."

"That's okay, Mom." I hate hearing the guilt in her voice. "Besides, you know my beets are better than yours anyway."

"Oh, they are not!" My mother is indignant.

"Bye, Mom."

"Go eat something, you ungrateful child."

I need mood music. I rifle through the CDs in the

living room until I find one of Mom's Spanish guitar CDs, and I turn it up. The liquid trail of notes makes me relax, and I wander back into the kitchen, ready to work.

Some people skin their beets before they roast them, but Mom always freaks when I do that. She swears all the vitamins to everything are right beneath the skin, so I just do a good job of scrubbing off the mud. I find four beets—two golden, two red—and lay them on a pan on top of a square of foil. After spritzing them with olive oil and adding a bit of sea salt, freshly ground pepper, and a few sprigs of rosemary from the plant in the window, I tuck the foil around the beets and slide them into the oven. Now I need something to entertain myself with for about an hour.

I plop on the couch, turn on the TV, and mute the sound. Then I hit speed dial. Since Mom doesn't have time to baby me, it's time to whine to Grandma.

It's just me and my mom that make up our immediate family and Mom's family is in the Bay Area. My dad, whom I barely remember, died in a car accident when I was three, and he was an only child, so when Grandma Muriel died last year, Mom and I lost a whole branch of our family tree. We're lucky to have MaDea, Mom's mom. "MaDea" isn't her real name (it's actually Emily Anita) but is more a Southern-flavored short for "mother dear" (and with a Louisiana drawl it sounds more like "mutha de-ah"), which is what a lot of Southern people in

41

Mom's generation call their mothers. Even when they're both on my last nerve, I consider myself lucky that I have the strong women in my family that I do.

MaDea has always treated me like I'm minor royalty, and going to her retirement village in Rossmoor to visit means I get to see all of Dea's friends—little old church ladies with great hats, orthopedic shoes, and purses full of peppermints for the "grandbaby." Every time we visit, Dea's friends give me their secret recipes, little gifts of silver dollars, old jewelry, and, usually, newspaper clippings from "Dear Abby" about all the things "girls my age" should avoid. Other girls might be "going to hell in a handbasket," but in my grandmother's opinion, I am more than perfect. A conversation with Dea is worth about a pound of chocolate as far as my ego is concerned.

"Hi, Dea!"

"It's my grandbaby! How are you?"

"I'm all right. How are you?" I settle back into the couch cushions with a blanket, waiting for my grandmother to update me on her "stories," the endless list of soap operas she watches.

"I'm just getting ready to head out the door," my grandmother says. "I'm going over to Eppie's next door to watch *Oprah*."

"Oh." I sniffle involuntarily. Is it just me, or does it

seem like even a seventy-three-year-old can find more of a social life than I can?

"Well, I won't keep you. I just wanted to say hi."

"I don't have to rush off. You sure you're all right?"

"I'm fine, Dee. I just have a little cold. I'm fixing some garlic, though."

"Oh, and some chicken soup. You know you should have some of that."

I swear, MaDea thinks chicken is a vegetable. There's no point in reminding her about "the vegetarian thing" unless I want to worry her. "Chicken soup. Right."

"Well, you get yourself some rest this weekend, you hear? Tell your mother I've got some sweet peas up here for you-all. Soon as it stops raining, you can put 'em out on your front porch."

"Okay, Dee. Have fun with *Oprah*."

"You take care, now. Be sweet."

"Yes, ma'am."

I flip channels awhile morosely. Friday afternoons used to be the best time of the week. Sim would come over for kindergarten, and we'd polish off leftovers from the restaurant while watching old movies to kick off the weekend. Other people have plans for the weekend and lives to lead. Why don't I have anything better to do?

I saw Sim at school today. He actually came to physics, which was a minor miracle, and while I was talking to Cheryl, he walked by my desk and knocked on it like he used to do when we were friends. It's weird. I keep wondering what he was going to say to me yesterday before Mom came in with the gingerbread. I'm still not sure why he came by. He said it was for gingerbread, but I still can't believe he really needed my notes. I wonder if it means something.

Stop, Lainey. Go cook something.

I've gotten good at cooking when I don't want to think about Sim anymore, when I need to fill up empty time and keep myself from drowning in my own head. My contest entries have more than doubled since he's been gone. Something good came out of being left alone long enough to get creative.

I'll make a new salad. Maybe Mom will put it on the restaurant menu.

Carefully, I take a soft, slippery head of roasted garlic out of the dish on the counter and slide it into the oven to warm through. Next, I open the fridge and find some salad greens to wash and tear. As I begin, I address an invisible studio audience with my best Martha Stewart impression.

"A small head of *butter* lettuce is preferable for this dish, but if you have a bit of leafy romaine, that will work just as well. Add to it a bit of arugula with the tough stems removed, some watercress for a peppery flavor, and maybe some mustard blossoms. If you don't have access to the fresh flowers, add some Dijon to your dressing, and you'll be surprised at what a difference it makes."

I snatch a mouthful of watercress and hum a bit of song from the CD. Maybe I'll use guitar music for my cooking show.

"Test and see if your beets are ready," I continue to lecture my audience as I open the oven and slide out the pan. I stick a fork into the biggest beet and decide it is done. "If they are, you'll want to add your garlic right away. If you want to skin your beets, wait until they cool, and rub the skin away and then proceed. However, if you want to preserve the vitamins below the skin, simply cut the beets into wedges and eat them skin on."

I grab a plate out of the dishwasher and assemble my salad. "Take your roasted garlic head, and squeeze out the buttery soft garlic onto the beets. When you're ready to plate, add your beets atop your salad greens and, with a little more salt, a little herbed chèvre"—I open the fridge again—"some slivered almonds, and, um . . . some Dijon dressing. Voilà! You have a beautiful, healthy, tasty salad."

I hold out my plate to my imaginary audience and then look at it critically. How are people supposed to use beets beautifully? Even dry-roasted, the red ones look a little gory. Maybe at my restaurant I'll only use golden beets or the red and white striped ones so it won't look like I've got gobbets of raw flesh in my salads. That's a good idea for a vegetarian restaurant anyway. I stab a

45

piece of lettuce with my fork and taste the dressing. The mustard is just strong enough.

I open the fridge to debate eating pasta or bread or pasta and bread. I'm scowling into the shelves when the phone rings. I'm pretty sure it's Mom—I swear my mother has an alarm that tells her when I've held the refrigerator door open for too long.

"Hi, Mom."

"I'm coming home, and guess what I've got," my mother singsongs.

"Fresh rolls?" I love Chef Pia's version of Vietnamese fresh rolls, full of bean thread noodles, mint, vegetables, and tofu.

"Nope. Something for your cold."

"Chicken soup!?"

"No, silly. Pumpkin."

"Pie?"

"You wish. Did you save me any of that pasta?"

"I just started on the beets."

"Good. The soup's still hot. It's fresh."

"Ooh, yum. Thanks, Mom, but you didn't have to leave work just for my cold."

"Sure I did," my mother says easily, releasing me from feeling guilty. "Anyway, it's the weekend. Who wants to work?"

LA SALLE ROUGE PUMPKIN CURRY SOUP

6 c. WATER

2 CUBES VEGETABLE BOUILLON

1 LARGE LEEK (WASH WELL!), HALVED AND SLICED CROSSWISE

4 c. PUREED PUMPKIN (KABOCHA SQUASH IS AWESOME; BUTTERNUT WILL WORK)

4 TBSP. CURRY

1 TSP. FRESHLY GRATED NUTMEG

5 THREADS SAFFRON

1/2 TSP. THYME

1 TSP. SALT

3/4 c. HEAVY WHIPPING CREAM

       ** USE HALF-AND-HALF TO LOWER FAT

12 OZ. EVAPORATED MILK

BOIL WATER, ADD BOUILLON, LEEKS. ADD PUMPKIN AND
SPICES. RETURN TO BOIL AND THEN SIMMER FOR
15-20 MINUTES UNTIL LEEKS HAVE SOFTENED. ADD
CREAM AND EVAPORATED MILK.

* <u>DO NOT BOIL AFTER ADDING CREAM</u> OR CREAM WILL CURDLE.

** SAINT JULIA ONCE SAID JACQUES PÉPIN WAS A "GARLIC FREAK," BUT USING A CLOVE OF CRUSHED, MINCED GARLIC WITH THIS IN ADDITION TO THE LEEK IS PRETTY TASTY TOO. SAINT JULIA ALSO SAID THAT USING A GARLIC PRESS IS A NO-NO! LAY A CLOVE DOWN ON YOUR CUTTING BOARD, LAY THE FLAT OF YOUR BIG KNIFE ON IT, AND WHACK IT WITH THE HEEL OF YOUR HAND. YOU CAN THEN PICK OUT THE PEEL AND EITHER MINCE IT OR ADD A LITTLE SALT AND RUB YOUR KNIFE IN IT; IT WILL SORT OF CRUSH AND MINCE ALL BY ITSELF.

** WASH YOUR HANDS WITH TABLE SALT TO TAKE AWAY THE SMELL. THIS WORKS!

4

Early Sunday morning, Mom and I head for Whole Earth Grocery. I think I could make a life's work out of going to the grocery store. Just the vivid colors of the produce, the salty tang of the seafood, the neat lines of bottled oils and vinegars, make me slow down and feel creative. Mom and I take about two hours to do the same pick-up-and-go type of shopping that takes most people fifteen minutes to do—mostly because we're scanning the produce aisles for anything new and checking out the seasonal varieties to see what's ripe. When Mom was working for the *Clarion,* we'd hit farmers' markets all over the county, usually bright and early Sunday mornings. Now we usually just hit our local market and find the extras cruising the store aisles.

I'm looking at tofu cream cheese and Mom's frowning, trying to decide between crème fraîche and Devon cream, when I hear someone call us.

"Vivi! Lainey! Hi!"

I cringe. It's Mrs. Hesseltine and her daughter, Lorraine. In elementary school, Lorraine and I used to be really good friends, but by the time we got to junior high, Lorraine figured that hanging around with a fat girl whose mother wouldn't give her a subscription to *Seventeen* wasn't good for her image. Lorraine is on her cell phone, looking reluctant to be in the store at all. I see her eyes sort of slide over me while her mother bustles up to us, waving.

"Hi, Tammy!" Mom brightens up and receives a hug. She and Mrs. Hesseltine used to be pretty close friends before Lorraine pulled her popular-person act and started being too cool to hang with me. I give Mrs. Hesseltine a lukewarm smile.

"Viv, it's so good to see you. And Elaine! You've really lost all of your puppy fat, haven't you?" Mrs. Hesseltine gushes. I cringe. *Puppy fat.* "Lorraine . . . ? Oh Lord, she's on the phone again." Mrs. Hesseltine looks aggravated. "I swear, I can't get her off of that thing for more than five minutes. Well, Elaine, how have you been? Lorraine says physics is giving her fits. Are you getting it? Maybe you girls can work together. . . ."

"Mom!" Lorraine is suddenly in the conversation. "I don't need a tutor."

And I don't want to tutor you either. I remember what

else I don't like about Lorraine. We used to be close friends until I figured out why she started hanging around at my house: Simeon. Every time he showed up, she turned into giggle girl and I turned into one person too many at my own house. What was really rough, though, was when she dropped me as a friend and started dating Sim the next week. Then it was like *both* of them had something better to do than hang out with me. I was really happy when Simeon dumped her. I never could figure out what he saw in her.

"I'm sure Elaine is hearing from all kinds of colleges—Lorraine is hoping for early admission to Stanford." Mrs. Hesseltine is still babbling, smiling at Mom. "You know, we should catch up sometime. Give me a call next week. I'd love to come by for lunch!"

I'm happy when Mrs. Hesseltine finally stops talking. At the rate we're going, we'll never get the groceries done, and I'm hoping Mom will have some time to hang out in the kitchen with me before she leaves for work. Everyone is exchanging pleasantries, and I mutter an unenthused, "Bye, Lorraine," when Mom pokes me with her elbow. All I want to do is get home.

"Why didn't you talk with Lorraine?" Mom asks as soon as we get away. I knew she would.

"She was on the phone, Mom," I say defensively. "I

know you think I don't make an effort, but I do. Lorraine and I aren't exactly friends anymore."

"I know," Mom says slowly. She glances over at me as she pushes the cart toward the checkout counter. "Sometimes I wonder if you don't need more of a social life, Lainey. Maybe you should get out some . . . do something fun. You know, the teen years just go by so fast. Next year you'll look back, and *whoosh!* you'll be diving into college, and it'll be over, and you'll have spent all your time with your old mom. We need to get you out there. I know Ana's boy is so friendly—I'm sure he would—"

"*Mom.*" All I need is to be paired up with "Ana's boy," Christopher Haines. Really, my life can get no worse. "*Please* don't start this again."

"I'm only making a suggestion," my mother says, looking resigned. "Lainey, I just wonder if you've gotten too isolated. Don't you keep up with any of your friends anymore?"

"I'm fine, Mom." I start unloading our cart onto the conveyor belt. "Everything's fine."

Smashing bananas was one of the first jobs Mom ever gave me to do in the kitchen when I was three, and I still do it by hand, with a fork, so the bananas in my banana bread are nice and chunky. Today I am doing it hard and fast, with violence.

It's a good thing banana bread is easy. I need something easy to make right now, something that doesn't take my total concentration and that will turn out well no matter what I do. Mom talked to me all the way home about "opening up to new experiences" and not "setting my standards for friendship unrealistically high." Where does she get this stuff?

I address my invisible audience again. "Place the banana purée into the bowl with the other wet ingredients and stir gently. If you need something to pulverize, you can crush your allspice with a handy mortar and pestle."

The cool stone pestle in my hand and the scent of the spices calm me a little. I know Mom means well, I do, but I feel freakish when she points out how different I am from other people in my class. Yeah, I know most of them would rather hang out in a crowd at the mall instead of in a restaurant kitchen, but I'm not like them, and I can't help it. Why does Mom expect me to be just like them and everyone else? Why isn't it enough that I'm me?

"If you'd like, you can add crushed pecans to the mix, but be sure to find all the bits and pieces of shell. Make sure your oven is heated to three-fifty, and divide your batter into two greased loaf pans. Set your timer for an hour, slide your loaf pans into the oven, and—voilà—you've got time for a quick cup of tea."

I'm just picking up the last of the banana peels from the counter and waiting for my water to boil when someone rings the bell downstairs.

Mom forgot her key. Sighing, I go to the security panel and press the button.

"Forget something?" I call into the intercom.

"It's me," says a familiar voice.

My jaw drops. I stand and listen to the buzzing in my ears.

"Laine?" His voice is tinny through the speaker.

"Uh, yeah, Sim." I push the button to unlock the lobby door. "Come on up."

Sim knocks again when he gets to the top of the stairs, and I open the door. He's standing there holding two cardboard cups from Soy to the World in a cardboard container. He holds one out to me.

"Chai?"

"Um, thanks." I wipe my hands on my jeans again and accept a cup awkwardly. Sim stands in the doorway waiting, his long black coat and boots spattered lightly with rain.

"Can I come in?"

Is this like vampires, when you have to invite them into the house?

I swallow and move back. "Sure."

The kettle starts screaming, and I'm startled into the

moment. I hurry into the kitchen and jerk it off the burner, nerves jangling. I fiddle with a sponge, turning it over in my hands, trying to get my brain organized, as he walks into my space and just waits.

"So, what—"

"What are you making?" Sim's sentence collides with mine, and I pause until he motions me to speak.

"Um . . . tea. Well, I was. And banana bread."

Sim bends and peers into the oven, shrugs out of his coat, and drops into a chair at the table. "Smells good."

I cradle my chai. "Yeah. Thanks for this, by the way."

"I thought I should bring something if I was just barging in."

"Yeah. Well, thanks."

"No problem."

I worry my bottom lip with my teeth, my stomach tight. The silence grows. In the past, I was comfortable with Sim in my house. Now it's been so long since he's been here that he seems awkward, misplaced, like something not meant for this room.

Simeon sips his tea and looks around, while I sip too big a gulp and scald my tongue. Eyes watering, I put down my cup and peer into the oven, just to be doing something. The top of the bread is golden, and I open the oven slightly, frowning. That was fast. I shrug and pull the pan out all the way.

"Man, that looks good."

I find a bamboo skewer and do the toothpick test. The bread seems pretty done, but . . . I gently press the top, then lean forward and inhale. It smells amazing.

"Is it done?"

"Mmm . . . I guess."

Simeon comes around the table to the counter. "So, are you cutting it, or is this for something special?"

"It's got to cool for twenty minutes."

"And then we're cutting it?"

I give Sim a look. "We?"

"Oh, c'mon." He regards me over the top of his chai cup. "You know I'm your best taste tester."

"Is that why you're here?"

Sim sets down his cup and crosses his arms, leaning against the table. "You know it. And to see what's up with you."

"What's up with me?" My voice rises. "What do you mean, *me*? What's up with *you*?"

Sim's eyebrows rise. "Whoa. I just meant, I wanted to see what you were doing. Don't get dramatic on me."

Immediately I'm angry, and just as quickly, I try to squash it. "Simeon . . . shut up, okay? I am not dramatic. You haven't just showed up here in, like, weeks. Since last semester."

"Yeah, well." Sim gives a dismissive shrug. "You know how it is. People get busy."

"Yeah, well," I mimic him, "people get sick of being blown off." Then I practically choke. I can't believe the words just came out of my mouth.

Simeon's eyebrows rise again. "Wow. I'm sorry, Laine. I didn't know you felt that way."

My face is prickling hot. How could he have not known I felt that way? "Yeah, well," I say again lamely, and turn back to the counter.

"Seriously." Sim reaches out and taps me on the shoulder. "I mean it, Laine."

I shrug. "It's okay."

"So, we're cool?" Sim taps me again.

"Yeah." The word comes out thickly. I'm embarrassed at how emotional a little apology makes me. I clear my throat and deliberately change the subject.

"We might as well go ahead and cut this, huh?"

"Yeah? Do we have ice cream?"

"We" again. "You know where it is."

The bread is far too hot and crumbly, and I can hardly make the slices come out of the pan intact. Saint Julia must be sighing deeply right now, but all I want to do is fill our mouths and stop talking. Hearing Simeon say he's sorry has me feeling oddly off balance, since he's not the type to apologize for anything. I want to be angry, to fight this out, but after an apology, it makes me look bad. It's hard to let it go.

I serve up a slice of banana bread in a bowl. Sim adds

a scoop of vanilla bean ice cream. We slide into seats at the kitchen table, spoons poised, and begin.

"What do you think?"

"It's good," Sim assures me around a mouthful of crumbs. "Not too sweet, good spiciness . . . I'd give it an eight out of ten."

"Only an eight? What's wrong with it?" I glance up sharply.

"Needs frosting." Sim smiles and shovels another bite into his mouth.

Right. Frosting. On *banana bread.* I roll my eyes. Sim is one of those people who put salt on their food before they taste it. In short, I don't know why I even asked.

Sim's spoon scrapes the bottom of his bowl. "I tell you I got a job?"

"No. Where?"

"At the little coffee shop near the Fourth Street freeway exit. They've got chai lattes."

"Soy? You're working at Soy to the World?" I frown and sip my drink. "Their chai is great, but their scones are awful. Why would you want to work there?"

Sim smacks his forehead. "I knew I'd forgotten something! At the interview, I meant to ask what the heck was up with their scones."

I catch myself smiling. "All right, don't start with me. What I mean is, why are you working?" The Kellers aren't stingy with their money. Sim has always had more stuff than anyone.

"I'm saving up for an apartment," Sim confides, taking another chunk of bread. "I'm thinking I'll move out by the end of the semester."

"An apartment? Huh." I twist my spoon. "Your parents are letting you?"

Sim makes an exasperated noise. "Letting me? Please. I'm eighteen in two months. They can't stop me."

Simeon takes another scoop of ice cream. "You know how it is, Laine—you just get to the point when you need your own space. I'm sick of my parents snooping around, treating me like I'm still some little kid. We just need some distance."

I nod a bit. I guess I can see needing distance from Sim's parents. In middle school, Mr. and Mrs. Keller were the type of parents that are all about their kids' winning—soccer games, spelling bees, and science fairs in elementary and junior high and, later, scholarship and essay contests. Sim has never really gotten into the competitive thing, and his laid-back "whatever" attitude drives his high-powered attorney father nuts.

"I remember your dad being pretty intense back in the day. Remember Little League?"

Sim grimaces. "Ugh, don't remind me. He argued with Coach so much he got me kicked out. He hasn't changed;

he's still all over me with the 'be a winner' thing. He said if I don't pull a 3.0 by midterm, he's thinking of sending me to military school for spring semester."

"Seriously? That's crazy! What does your mom think about it?"

"My mother has been out in the desert with some meditation retreat thing. She's coming back next week, and she 'wants to share the changes in her life,' blah blah blah. It's going to be a freaking nightmare."

"It sounds unreal," I say.

"You have no idea," Sim groans. "She wants all of us to have our chakras aligned. You know what that might do to my social life?"

"I won't even ask."

Sim keeps talking. Little by little, the knotted, tense feeling in my stomach goes away. It's like the last semester never happened. We sit and eat, and Sim talks about people I don't know, but I don't really care. I'm just glad he's here.

We're carefully polite. When Sim's cell phone battery dies, I offer to let him use my charger upstairs. Sim says he'll go as soon as he's got "juice," and he politely sits on the floor in the hallway to wait.

"You can come in," I tell him. I hand him the remote. "Here. Find a movie or something."

Sim flips a few channels and finds an ancient episode

of *Buck Rogers*. We laugh at the bad seventies hairdos, and things start to feel more normal. While I go get more banana bread, Sim gets comfortable, stretching out on my double bed. He pulls off his sweatshirt and his boots and gets crumbs on my comforter.

"Did you just spill *milk* on my bed?" I ask as I catch him furtively blotting at something with his shirttail.

"No, no, it's just on my shirt." Sim skins out of it and tosses it on the floor. "See? Got it."

"You're such a slob," I say, and get up to get him another sweatshirt. "Here."

"No, I'm going in a minute," Sim says, waving his hand so I'll quit blocking the TV. "As soon as this show goes off."

"Right."

And that's how Mom finds us, hours later—Sim in my bed with the covers up to his chest (when did he do that?) and me, sprawled fully clothed right beside him, the plate of banana bread crumbs trapped between us, watching TV with barely open eyes.

"Lainey?" My mother comes up the stairs. "Did you notice . . . *Elaine?*" Mom's voice skips an octave up the scale and my body flings itself upright.

THE BEST BANANA BREAD

1 C. WHOLE WHEAT PASTRY FLOUR (ADDS FIBER, CUTS CARBS)

1 C. WHITE FLOUR

1/4 C. BROWN SUGAR

1 C. CHOPPED PECANS (TOTALLY OPTIONAL)

2 TSP. BAKING POWDER

1 TSP. BAKING SODA (NECESSARY - OTHERWISE IT WON'T RISE RIGHT)

1/2 TSP. SALT

1? C. SMASHED BANANAS (ABOUT 3)

1 EGG

2/4 C. APPLESAUCE (REPLACES THE OIL)

2 TSP. LEMON ZEST

1 TSP. VANILLA EXTRACT

1 TSP. ALLSPICE (YOU CAN EXCHANGE FOR CINNAMON
                    BUT - LIVE A LITTLE. TRY A NEW SPICE!)

IN A MEDIUM-SIZED BOWL, PULL TOGETHER THE FIRST 7 (DRY) INGREDIENTS. SET ASIDE.

IN A SMALL BOWL, COMBINE THE REMAINING INGREDIENTS AND STIR. MIX TOGETHER THE DRY AND THE WET INGREDIENTS A LITTLE AT A TIME. POUR INTO (2) 8x4x3 INCH LOAF PANS THAT HAVE BEEN SPRAYED WITH NONSTICK SPRAY. BAKE AT 350°F FOR ABOUT 1 HOUR OR UNTIL A TOOTHPICK INSERTED IN THE CENTER COMES OUT CLEAN. MAKES

ABOUT 12 SLICES.

* * SAINT JULIA TIP: YOU CAN USE LEMON JUICE
INSTEAD OF LEMON ZEST IF YOU DON'T HAVE IT.
ALSO, ADDING CHOPPED DATES OR RAISINS CAN
MAKE UP FOR LEAVING OUT THE NUTS.

5

"Oh, hi, Mom!"

My voice doesn't sound normal. It's too high. I clear my throat and wish I could start over again. Stay calm, Mom. It's nothing. Honest.

"What's up, Mrs. Seifert." Simeon yawns. He sits up and rubs his face for a moment, then blinks. There is an awkward silence.

My mother is standing in the doorway, very still, her arms down at her sides, her fingers rolling the red piping on the edges of her white chef's jacket. Sim pulls back the covers and climbs out of my bed, markedly casual as he shrugs into his milk-damp shirt and steps into his shoes. He grabs his sweatshirt. "I guess I'd better get some homework done before work tonight, huh?"

I would laugh, except I can see that Mom is on the knife edge of being upset. Simeon never does homework; we all know that.

I can see conflict clashing across my mother's face. Why is Simeon in her daughter's bed? Should she ask him to stay? Should she hurry him away? What's going on?

"We're just watching old sci-fi," I babble to fill the silence. "*Buck Rogers* . . . you know. Bad costumes."

"I see." She directs her dark glance at me, riffling her fingers through her cropped natural hair and sighing. I can read words in her expression. *Elaine Seifert, you will explain this later.*

"You're on at five-thirty?" I ask Simeon, turning slightly toward him.

"Yep. You coming out?"

I glance at my mother. She doesn't look like she's up to me going across town to hang out at Sim's new job. Not tonight.

"Nah. See you tomorrow, huh?"

"Right. Bye, Mrs. S."

"It was so good to see you, Simeon," my mother says tiredly, then her genteel Southern instinct bursts forth in ultra-politeness. "Please don't rush off on my account. I brought back some fresh rolls from the restaurant."

Simeon grins. He knows when he's got my mother off balance. "I think I've cleaned you out of sweets again," he says, giving her a charming glance that never fails to thaw her. "I'd better go while you might still let me come back."

My mother, predictably, gives a wry smile and shakes her head. Today, though, her smile doesn't quite reach her eyes as she turns back toward me.

Sim thanks me for the banana bread and finishes buttoning his shirt as my mother's glance goes from my bed to me to the boy who is leaving my bedroom and back to me. As soon as Simeon is gone, I can look forward to Vivianne Seifert's Twenty Questions. I can tell Sim feels the vibe too, 'cause he's gone before I know it. Coward.

I've said before that Mom is pretty cool. I know she's reminding herself of this fact as she unbuttons the red cloth fastenings on her chef's jacket. Her fingers move slowly, and I can practically hear her plotting how this should go.

Mother: Tell me everything.

Daughter: Oh, Mother dear, of course!

"So . . . it's nice to see Sim around," my mother says conversationally.

Mom's sermons are always worse when she starts out so calmly. "Yeah. It was good to hang out. He has a job now at that coffee shop, Soy to the World."

"That's good. . . ." Mom trails off, clears her throat. "Elaine, I'm . . . a little concerned with what I saw today. I'm going to make some guidelines. About visits."

"Visits?" I tilt my head and try a look of polite curiosity, feeling the blood coming to my face. "We're just hanging out, like always."

Mom levels a glance at me. "I can appreciate that. It was good to see you with a friend over. . . ." Her voice trails away. "Your friends are always welcome here, but as it stands, we need to make some rules for now."

"Rules? Mom."

"Elaine," Mom says warningly. "Old friends or not, I . . . well, I was caught a little off guard by . . . by a boy in your bed with no shirt on."

"He always takes off his shoes over here."

"Elaine."

I sigh. "He spilled something on his shirt."

"All right—" Mom lifts a placating hand. "Fine. That's not the issue. But I think . . ." Mom clears her throat, plunges in. "Honey, we still need some guidelines. I know"—Mom waves her hand over my objections—"that you don't need to have the little talk I gave you in the fifth grade. I just want you to be clear in your own head, Elaine, what's going on. You don't want to have any . . . regrets . . . about your friendship now that things have changed between you two. . . ."

"They *haven't*," I snap, my ears heating up. "It's not like that. Sim doesn't see me like that." As soon as the words are out, I wish them back. My mother is looking at me with a little worried furrow in her forehead, her eyes getting all shiny and soft with pity.

"Oh, *Lainey,* honey, you're such a beautiful girl," she begins, and tentatively reaches out a hand.

There is nothing more lame than my parent apologizing because I *don't* have a love life for her to worry about. I hold out my arm, stiff, to ward her off. "*Mom.* Please."

My mother straightens and blows out a sigh. "Well, Elaine, here's the bottom line: I'm glad that you and Simeon are friends; you know I've always liked him, and I want your friends to be welcome in our home. However, I would prefer if when you two come over here that you stay . . . downstairs."

I shrug like I don't care, but I can barely lift my face. How humiliating. I have so little social life that I don't need to have a curfew. Now Mom doesn't have to give me rules about Simeon, but she's doing it anyway.

"I'm sorry if this is embarrassing," Mom says like she's reading my mind. "Simeon is welcome to come here anytime, and when he visits, I know you guys will have fun. I'd just feel better if I didn't have to come upstairs to find you and wonder . . . what you'd been doing."

I grind my teeth, wishing she'd shut up. "We weren't doing anything. This is so unnecessary."

"Elaine," my mother says tiredly, "give me some credit for knowing a little about human nature. You weren't doing anything today, but another day, who knows? When I was your age—"

I sigh, feeling my shoulders slump in defeat. In high school, my mother had tons of friends, bunches of boyfriends, and a life totally different from mine. She always brings up her life like it has something to do with me. When Mom talks about her big homecoming-queen high school days, I feel stupid. This isn't *necessary*. It's like I'm six and my mom's still arranging my playdates, telling me what I can and can't do when she's not there to watch. Even when she's not watching, nothing is going on with Sim and me. *Nothing.*

"Well." Mom realizes she's started reminiscing, and her voice fades. She clears her throat. "Look, let's drop this, okay? How about we split a piece of that banana bread? Did you use up all my pecan bark?" My mother trails off, turning toward the kitchen.

"Wait a second, Mom." I clear my throat. "I'm not hungry, and I need to say this."

I don't want any food. That's how I always used to deal with things.

When I used to skin my knees, Mom would give me a cupcake. When the first boy I ever liked threw rocks at me in the second grade, Mom taught me how to make

69

frosting. Pretty soon I made frosting every time I felt bad. And I ate it. Now whenever Mom and I argue, we split something. A bite of bread, a piece of cake, a bar of chocolate. It's a little sugar to make the bitterness ease. If Mom and I can't eat together, she gets worried.

Sometimes it's hard to resist being given treats like a little kid. Everyone wants to be comforted, to have the hurt taken out of a fight. But food makes a sloppy bandage.

"Look, whether you believe me or not"—I face my mother—"I'm telling the truth. Sim just spilled something. It was totally innocent. We are not getting involved. But if it makes you feel happy to make up rules for your daughter, who isn't actually dating the guy without a shirt on, who was under her covers alone, without her, then fine: we'll watch TV downstairs from now on, okay? With our *coats* on."

Mom's eyebrows lower. "Watch your tone, Elaine." She exhales and rubs her hands against her face. "Look, I didn't mean to infer . . . I know he's not your boyfriend, but I also know how boys . . . Well." She takes a breath, shaking her head. "Let's save that for another time. So, Simeon liked the banana bread."

I sigh and change gears. "Yeah. I didn't use the pecan bark, and the sugar substitute really worked out well. Sim couldn't tell the difference." I clear my throat and try to relax my shoulders.

Mom shrugs out of her chef's jacket and walks toward her bedroom. "Good. Oh, I meant to tell you . . ." I unfold myself from the bed and follow as she keeps talking. "We've been experimenting with the gingerbread you started the other day. If I don't add any crystallized ginger, I could use it on our light-dessert menu."

"Yeah? I think you should do it. With a tiny bit of that ginger-carrot sorbet, that would be awesome. Or maybe you could just have an ice cream sandwich?"

"Oh, good idea! And I could just put it on the regular menu, with the ginger ice cream, and it would be a 'half the sugar' dessert; we could roll the edges in some chopped crystallized ginger."

I flop down on Mom's bed and envision the dessert, plated on the square red dessert plates . . . a dusting of powdered sugar and sprig of mint . . . perfect. I imagine having my own show, where how you plate something can make the difference between a dish that's a dud and a dish that wins you national acclaim. For Saint Julia, it was a simple omelet—a big "French" food to Americans back in the sixties. For me, who knows? Someday I'm going to make this gingerbread for someone who can take me to the top.

Mom pokes her head around the edge of the closet. "Well, I came home in the first place to see if I could pick you up for dinner tonight. . . . Pia made hot and sour soup, and there's always fresh rolls, of course."

"I'm coming down to the restaurant, but I'm walking. I ate a *bunch* of bread today."

Mom sighs. "Lainey. You are a size-fourteen woman of African American descent. This is not unheard of in Western civilization. Eating bread will not kill you. Lord, I *knew* I should've never let you play Barbies."

I close my eyes. "Mom . . ."

My mother worries that I'm going to end up with some eating disorder. This after I lost only four sizes in two long years of trying. I've got Mom's height (five foot four) but my father's big bones, wide shoulders, and flat butt, plus Mom's high waist, big bust, and skinny legs, which, unless I work at it, gives me the figure of Humpty Dumpty on toothpicks. Mom and Pia are two of the best chefs that I know, and I am not about to miss out on that. However, I know my body, and I know that if I let bread sit too long, sugar free or not, it's going to stick. I've already been the tubby freshman, thank you. No need to carry that into college to add to the freshman fifteen.

"Look, Barbie Junior, I'll tell you what—I'll walk with you. Pia can drop us home after the dinner rush."

I make a face. "And I'll have to lug my laptop and all of my books?"

My mother sighs. "Fine."

"You know what other kind of dessert you could make?" I say, placating her sense of motherly duty.

"Carrot macaroons! See, these are the kinds of thoughts I have when I walk. Now, I'd be depriving you of my great cognitive abilities if I just sat in the car with you, did you know that?"

My mother groans and pushes me out of her bedroom. "Go away, child. Carrot macaroons is taking your healthy-desserts thing just a *little* too far."

"I'll make some tonight!" I holler through the door.

I hear the sound of the shower and smile.

It's a quick walk to the restaurant on a Sunday evening, and I kind of walk, kind of jog to get there. Mom's in her office when I finally go down, showing the new "busboy" how to tie her red silk tie in the traditional half-Windsor knot the waitstaff use. The girl looks rushed but smiles at me as she leaves, wrapping her long white apron around her black slacks. I laugh when I settle into Mom's desk chair and look at the notes on her computer.

"I thought you didn't like my idea for carrot macaroons."

Mom sighs and rolls her eyes. "I was trying to get it out of my mind. My *Southern Melodies* cookbook has a recipe that uses a cup of mashed carrots, but I haven't found anything I like in the macaroon category." Mom shrugs. "If you can find me something that works, I'll put your name to it in the menu."

"What's the special tonight?" I ask as my mother buttons herself into the white silk jacket she wears during dinner. It isn't anything I would cook in, but Mom mostly walks around smiling and schmoozing, and the coat, with its double row of knotted frog fastenings, rarely gets dirty. Mom has four of them just in case one does.

"I think we've got a garlic squid pasta," Mom says, pulling out the low chef's toque she wears with the formal chef's jacket, "and Pia's said something about a pecan-encrusted catfish. The soup is white asparagus with prawn and coconut milk, a little spicy, very warming for this nippy evening, a nice pumpkin curry soup as well . . . and then there's the usual."

I nod, trying to keep my face still as I think of squid pasta. Bleeuch. In my cooking show of the future, we'll only have vegetarian dishes. To me, animals are pretty much either too ugly to consider eating or too cute to imagine dead.

"I'll come up for some of Pia's fresh spring rolls later on. I've got to finish a paper."

Mom doesn't look at me. "If you'd like, we can run by Sim's job, that Soy World place, after the rush is over and have some coffee."

I blink.

My mother turns back toward the closet, rummaging for her lipstick. "Only if you want to," she goes on. "And if it wouldn't bother him."

I bite my lip, considering. Mom is still bugged by the whole Sim thing, and I can't tell where she's going with it. Does she think I need her to come with me to see him?

"Maybe another time," I say uncomfortably. "I really should work on this paper."

Mom turns back around, fiddling with an eyelash curler. "All right," she says absently. "Another time, then. It was just a thought." She closes the closet door and does a turn. "Do I pass?" She gestures at her outfit.

I nod. "You look fine."

"All righty, then. See ya." My mother gives a quick wave and steps out.

I drop my chin into my palm and frown at the door.

My mother is driving me nuts. She's constantly saying I don't have enough friends, then the minute one comes over, she starts making rules about how we can hang out. Now she's taking a huge interest in Simeon— and wants to hang out and watch him work? I can't say I like how this feels. I have no idea what my mother's up to. But when it's my mother? It can't be good.

MA DEA'S PECAN BARK

1 ¾ C. PECANS, CHOPPED
1 C. BROWN SUGAR, PACKED
1 TSP. CINNAMON, OPTIONAL
DASH OF SALT — MAYBE ⅛ TSP.
DASH OF CAYENNE, OPTIONAL
1 C. UNSALTED BUTTER (NOTE: THIS IS ALREADY NOT A HEALTH
                                          FOOD ITEM!)

PREHEAT OVEN TO 350° F.

LINE A COOKIE SHEET WITH WAXED PAPER, AND GREASE
IT THOROUGHLY. EVENLY SPRINKLE PECANS OVER THE PAN.
MIX TOGETHER [SALT] BROWN SUGAR, CINNAMON, AND CAYENNE, IF YOU'RE ADDING IT.
IN A HEAVY-BOTTOMED SAUCEPAN, MELT THE UNSALTED
BUTTER. ADD BROWN SUGAR [MIXTURE] LITTLE BY LITTLE TO THE PAN,
STIRRING THOROUGHLY, UNTIL ALL THE SUGAR IS ADDED,
AND THE MIXTURE BEGINS TO BUBBLE.

USING A HEAT-PROOF SPATULA, * CAREFULLY * POUR THE
LAVA-SUGAR MIXTURE OVER THE NUTS. BAKE FOR
10 MINUTES, THEN REMOVE FROM THE OVEN AND COOL
ON THE COUNTER FOR 10 MINUTES. PLACE PAN IN
THE FREEZER FOR ONE HOUR. BREAK INTO
BITE-SIZED PIECES WHEN COOLED.

** FOR PECAN BARK BARS: LINE THE PAN WITH GRAHAM CRACKER SQUARES OR PECAN SHORTBREAD, THEN ADD NUTS AND SUGAR MIXTURE. TASTY!

6

"Hey, so, was your mom okay last night? You're not in trouble with her or anything, are you?" To my happy surprise, Sim is waiting at my desk in physics the next day.

I can barely keep a smile off my face. "No. Mom's cool. You know how she is."

"Yeah." Sim nods, relieved. "Look. You know that stuff you guys got when your grandma died? Think your mom would care if I took some of it?"

"No . . ." I make a face, imagining the boxes crammed into the guest room closet. "Why?"

Sim grins and lowers his voice. "I got my place last night."

"No way!"

"Way." Simeon leans close. "It's two blocks from Soy, and until Dad gives back my car or I buy one, I can take the bus from a block away. It's gonna happen, Laine."

"That's amazing! I can't believe you set this up so fast!"

"Incoming," Cheryl interrupts quietly. Mr. Wilcox is advancing on us with his usual jovial expression of good cheer.

"Mr. Keller, how nice of you to join us today," Mr. Wilcox booms. Sim rolls his eyes and moves over to the next aisle as Mr. Wilcox continues, "If we could get started, people . . ."

For the rest of class, I've got a little glow. I'm really happy for Sim, and I can't wait to see his new apartment. He is so lucky. Even though I love my room and my house, I know it'd also be cool to have my own place for real. I can't believe Sim's parents are cool enough to let him do this. *My* mother would have a conniption fit.

I'm halfway home after school when Sim catches up with me again.

"Hey, you!"

"Hey!" I turn around and give a ridiculously pleased smile.

"So, I'm already packed." Sim grins back, dropping a companionable arm around my shoulders. He picks up the conversation where he left off this morning. "I'm trying to decide if I should wait to leave until my mother comes home and conveniently remembers it's almost my birthday, or should I just sort of vanish before anyone's looking for me?" He gives a wicked laugh. "I should be

taking bets on how many days it'll take for them to figure out that I'm not home. What do you think, Laine?
Two days? Or three?"

Sim's arm is still around me, and I look up into his
face. "Wait, what? Your parents don't know you're moving out?"

"What did I just say?" He's still grinning, with that
manic light in his eyes.

I stop. "Man, *that's* going to freak them out. Your
mom's going to start calling hospitals and morgues. Then
your dad's going to call his friends on the police force."

"The cops won't do anything for something like
twenty-four hours." Sim smiles angelically. "And I'm not
breaking any laws; I'll come home once a week so they
can't say I've actually moved until I fill out the emanci-
pation paperwork or I turn eighteen. As far as they're
concerned, I'm not a missing person—I just . . . moved."

Shaking my head, I fish out my keys, unlock the
lobby door, and begin the climb to our floor. "You totally
screw with your parents' minds, Sim, you know that?"

"Yeah, well, they shouldn't have started screwing
with me. It's not like they don't deserve it."

"Jeez, Sim . . ." I drop my backpack and close the
door behind us.

Simeon rolls his eyes, his mood evaporating lightning-
quick. "*Jeez, Sim,*" he imitates me. He flops onto the

couch in our front room and takes out a battered brass lighter, flipping open its lid and spinning around the small canister so that the flame appears as a blur. Even though he says he quit smoking, Sim still has tons of what I call stupid lighter tricks. He does one while he talks.

"My mom's going to get back from her retreat or whatever, and then, at the last minute, she'll remember it's almost my birthday, and then she'll make a big deal of it, and then she'll start talking about what a beautiful baby I was and how I was such a lovable little fellow and all the neighbors were jealous, and then she'll get all emotional because I'm such a disappointment to her now, blah blah blah."

"Well . . ." I don't know what to say. I plop down next to him, feeling uncomfortable, as I always do when I think about Sim's family. His parents really don't get him. He's sensitive and artistic and unique, but he's not a perfectionist or all into grades and "achievements," so they don't know how to treat him.

"It's not like they haven't been pushing for this, Laine," Sim continues. "They probably want me to leave anyway . . . and you know what? One of these days, I'm just gonna go."

Flip. Flip. Sim's flipping the flame on and off. On and off.

Every single magazine or novel or movie about high school has kids in it being mouthy, and parents putting up with it, until suddenly the kids are off to college and everyone misses each other and the credits roll for the Family Channel holiday movie. How come it's never really like that in real life?

"That would suck," I say finally.

Sim shrugs.

"I would miss you," I admit, and Sim shrugs again.

"And," I continue, ignoring his lack of response, "no matter how crappy they treat you, I think your parents would miss you too, Sim."

"Right." Sim's voice is lifeless, his eyes flat. "Since I'm not 'living up to my potential' and I'm such a 'big disappointment,' I'm sure they would be dying for me to come back. Right."

"Remember at the seventh-grade science fair, when you got disqualified for not having your whole project with you? And then you walked home to get the part you'd left, and your parents thought you'd been kidnapped?"

Sim cracks a smile at that. "Seventh grade. Those were the days, man."

"Your parents freaked, Sim. Your mom cried when you came back. Remember?"

Flip. Flip. Simeon looks at me and shrugs. "That was a long time ago, okay? My parents can't do anything to stop me from going," he continues, flipping the lighter faster in some complicated, over-the-knuckles move. "I already know that I'm not what they want, so why not make it easier on everybody and go?"

There's nothing to say to that. His parents are messed up, and that's not going to change, but I know that saying this won't help. I fumble to change the subject.

"It's almost four. We'd better get to kindergarten." I put my hand on the lighter, grabbing his arm when he tries to shake me off. "Let's go see what food Emeril is shouting at today." Anything is better than watching Sim get depressed.

Simeon shrugs again, then stands, shoving the lighter into his pocket and fiddling with his silver snake ring. "Nah . . . Let's go see if your grandma had any decent curtains." He smiles wryly. "She's got to have something better than the pink flowery ones I saw at the Catholic thrift shop."

"Grandma's stuff is in the guest room," I say quickly, relieved I can do something to help. "Come on."

When I crack open the first box, I can smell Grandma Muriel's perfume—a kind of powdery lavender smell. I stop and breathe it in, feeling almost guilty giving her things to Sim—I know she meant me to have them, and Mom said I should keep some of this stuff for college. But I don't need it right now, and Sim does.

As it turns out, Simeon hasn't thought much about

rugs, sheets, or towels, not to mention the curtains he was after. Or pots and pans, either. He doesn't even have a couch, but he has found a double mattress and a box spring, and he figures he'll use his camping gear—a little gas stove and a sleeping bag—until his paycheck from Soy kicks in.

"You're using a gas stove? Your apartment doesn't have a stove?" I squeak.

"I think it has one," Sim says, "it just doesn't have an oven. I'll get a microwave. It'll be fine."

"I couldn't live without a stove."

"Sure you could. You could say, 'Hey, it's camping!' And you'd be fine."

"We can do better than you camping," I tell him.

I pile a couple of sets of sheets, some plain brown curtains, two of Grandma's rag rugs, and some old, but still reasonably thick, towels on the floor. Simeon, sitting on the bed, gives me the thumbs-up or thumbs-down on everything I pull out.

"No, Sim, that bedspread is hideous," I argue as he gives me a thumbs-up on some tufted chenille thing and puts it in his pile. "No one in their right mind would ac- tually be able to sleep under that. Here. Put it in the 'to go' pile. Maybe someone can make a quilt out of it."

Simeon thinks Grandma's stuff is great—his word is *retro*. I think it's hilarious.

"You just don't understand art when you see it," Simeon insists. "That, tacked to the wall, would make a killer background for posters or something. Trust me on this, Lainey. You have no idea how much I'm feeling this."

I sigh. I know I have no idea. My room is what reflects my mom's idea of décor. Up until now, that has worked out okay, because I don't usually care what things look like as long as there's enough light to read by and plenty of pillows for when I want to prop up and watch TV. Now the navy blue sheets, denim accent pillows with their white buttons, and white-striped duvet and matching window seat look hopelessly buttoned down and little girlish. Even the signed picture Pia got me of Saint Julia and Jacques Pépin, framed and in the place of honor above my dresser, seems kind of babyish.

Sim reads my thoughts. "I'll do your room next," he consoles me, and I make a face.

"Oh no, you won't. I don't do chenille."

"Just wait. You'll be begging me," Sim says cheerfully. "Better say yes now," he adds. "After next week, I'll start charging."

"Whatever!" I throw a pillowcase in the direction of his head.

We pack up two boxes of stuff for Sim and lug them downstairs. "You want anything to eat?" I ask him as he flops on the couch in the den and picks up the remote.

"Whatcha got?" he asks. He has his phone in hand, punching numbers.

"Just some leftovers from the restaurant," I say, investigating the contents of the refrigerator. "We've got soup and rolls and half a cheesecake."

Sim grunts and starts talking on the phone. I bring him a slice of dessert and a fork. He keeps talking, arranging with someone to pick up the boxes, gossiping about someone at school, taking bites, and nodding. He keeps his hand on the TV remote, flipping channels and talking. He flips past a cooking show.

"Hey!" I grab the remote.

Sim rolls his eyes and keeps talking.

It's another chef with a band in her kitchen (where do they get these people?), but I watch the cooking show anyway and learn how to make grape focaccia. Unbelievably, Sim stays on the cell phone the whole time. He talks until he's finished the rest of the cheesecake and the credits are rolling down the screen. When he hangs up, I'm a little annoyed.

"So, I guess the cheesecake was good," I say, indicating the empty pan.

"What? Oh yeah, it was great. Listen, Jared's on his way over, and he's going to drop me home, so I'll see ya, okay?"

"Oh." Disappointment coagulates in my stomach. "Um, okay. Let me know if you need anything else."

Sim leans over and gives me a one-armed hug. "Thanks, Laine. As soon as I get settled, I promise I'm making you dinner. You'll be my first guest."

"Really?" I laugh and hug him back, disappointment lifting a little. "What, so, we're having toast?"

"I can cook!" Sim insists. He taps his finger on my nose, eyes narrowed in mock anger. "You'll be sorry you doubted me."

I can't stop smiling. "Fine. You cook, but I'm making dessert."

"Oh, can you make some of that cheesecake?" Sim brightens. "Is it hard to—"

Simeon's eyes leave mine at the sound of the downstairs buzzer, and he's off the couch and heading for the door before I can recover.

"'S'up, Jared?" he says into the intercom. "On my way."

I stand in the lobby with my hands in my pockets, looking at the little SUV pulled up on the front walk. I've seen the girl in the car at school. Her name is Serena or something. She gives me a little nod from behind her sunglasses. She is skinny and glamorous, her blond-streaked hair razor cut and tousled. I feel immature with my ponytail and jeans.

Sim opens the back door. "Okay, thanks, Lainey, see ya," he says.

"No problem," I say, swallowing. Sim and his friends head off down the street, and I go back inside with a little sigh. I wish Sim would've stuck around a little longer, but if I'm being real, I know he only came over here for Grandma Muriel's stuff anyway. That and the leftovers he ate. I pick up the empty pie plate and stare at it. Whoever said that the way to a man's heart was through his stomach doesn't know Sim. He's been eating over here forever, and I'm not any closer to his heart, especially not lately.

And then I remember that he's making me dinner.

I smile and set the cheesecake pan in the sink. It won't take me long to cook up another one.

QUICK AND EASY CHEESECAKE
WITH LEMON SAUCE

24 OZ. CREAM CHEESE
1 - 1/2 C. SUGAR
3 EGGS
2 TSP. LEMON RIND
GRAHAM CRACKER CRUST (STORE-BOUGHT)

BLEND CREAM CHEESE, SUGAR, EGGS, AND LEMON RIND
UNTIL SMOOTH. POUR INTO PRE-MADE GRAHAM CRACKER
CRUST AND BAKE AT 350°F FOR 50 MINUTES OR
UNTIL BARELY FIRM (IT'LL FIRM THE REST OF THE WAY ON
THE COUNTER). SERVE WITH STORE-BOUGHT LEMON
CURD, OR YOU CAN MAKE YOUR OWN:

EASY LEMON SAUCE

1/2 C. SUGAR
1/4 TSP. SALT
1 C. BOILING WATER
1 TBSP. CORNSTARCH (PLUS 1 TBSP. COLD WATER)
2 TBSP. LEMON PEEL, FINELY GRATED
1/4 C. FRESH-SQUEEZED LEMON JUICE
1 TBSP. BUTTER

IN A SAUCEPAN, COMBINE SUGAR AND SALT. ADD
BOILING WATER. MIX CORNSTARCH AND COLD WATER,
AND ADD TO THE MIX. COOK, STIRRING CONSTANTLY,
UNTIL MIXTURE IS THICK AND CLEAR, STIR IN
LEMON PEEL, LEMON JUICE, AND BUTTER. SERVE WARM
OVER CHEESE CAKE SLICES.

* * MELTED ORANGE MARMALADE IS GOOD ON
     CHEESECAKE TOO.

7

I'm so inspired by my cheesecake idea that I make mini-cheesecakes for the entire group in Vocal Jazz. Since I'm making so many, I cheat and use store-bought mini–graham cracker crusts, which isn't what I normally do, but it's worth it to be able to bring them to class and pass them around. Ms. Dunston says she'll take the extras to the faculty lounge and tell everyone that I made them, which means I'd better get an A+ on every single paper I turn in today.

I'm in such a great mood that I don't even mind that one of those weird nonword jazz songs, "Oo-Shoo-Be-Doo-Be," is playing, and Ms. Dunston is going to make us work on "Java Jive" for the spring concert. Not even goofy songs about coffee addicts can ruin things for me. As Ms. Dunston talks about diction before warming us up, I overhear Ben whispering to Tracey.

"So, Keller's this weekend. You going?"

"I just heard about it."

Did he say "Keller's"? I lean forward slightly.

"So, is it his brother's birthday or something?"

"Uh . . ." Ben leans back. "Just a party, I think. First one in the new place and all."

A party? In someone's new place? Is Sim having a party? Why hasn't he mentioned it?

"Let's take it from the top, please," Ms. Dunston is saying, and I stand automatically and open my music.

I guess I'm not going to be his first guest.

Not that it matters, if it's true. Not really. I mean, it's no big deal, right? He obviously has other friends; I've always known that. So, I'll be his second guest. Anyway, I don't know the details. I can always ask him in physics.

For once, Vocal Jazz seems to go on forever, and I'm hurrying toward physics class instead of dragging my feet.

"Hey, what's up?" Cheryl asks, rattling her bag of sunflower seeds in my direction.

"Not much," I reply, looking toward Sim's place. I glance at the door and see other students coming in. The warning bell hasn't even rung yet. He has lots of time.

"So, did you see the box on Wilcox's desk?" Cheryl asks.

"Oh no. Are those springs? Today is lab again already?"

"Yep. How much you wanna bet we're going to have

to measure the springs and then write down any 'lingering questions' we have about them?" Cheryl laughs.

The warning bell rings, and Mr. Wilcox comes into the room. Sim only has two minutes left, and I'll barely have a chance to talk to him.

"If you're looking for Sim," Cheryl offers, "I saw him on the steps of the ad building, on his way to the parking lot with Levi Pressman."

"Oh." I turn from the door reluctantly. Sim is cutting again.

Cheryl leans forward to catch my eye. "So, partners again?"

I look at her and smile weakly. "What? Oh yeah. Sure."

It is a long, slow hour. Even Mr. Wilcox telling me at the end of class that he appreciated tasting my cheesecake doesn't do much for my mood. Then at lunch I run into Christopher Haines, and the first words out of his mouth are:

"Did you hear about Simeon Keller's party?"

"Why do you want to know?" I realize how close to a snarl I am. I try to soften up with an insincere smile. "Are you going?"

Christopher shrugs, scrunching his hands into the pockets of his jeans. "Everybody is," he says lamely.

Right. Everybody. I heave a huge sigh. "Whatever,

Chris. Look, I've really got to study." I bury myself in my reading for English lit the rest of the meal.

By the time school's over, it seems like the whole student body knows about Sim and Carrigan Keller's party, even outside the people I know from junior high. And it seems like the entire student body is invited, even Christopher Haines, who is a complete wannabe and isn't even all that close friends with either Carrigan or Sim. I don't get any of this. Yeah, Sim has the right to hang with his loser brother, have a party, and ask anyone he wants. But would it have killed him to mention it, maybe say, "Hey, Laine, I'm throwing a bash at the house, maybe stop by"? Is something wrong with me? Why didn't he ask?

Is it stupid to be upset about this? Yes. Am I upset anyway? Yes.

I go straight into the restaurant kitchen after school, and instead of helping Gene wash radishes for salad prep, I go straight for the onions and chop for thirty minutes before I get to my homework. That way, when tears blur my eyes and I have to keep stopping to wipe my face, it's just the onions making me weep. As I chop, the heavy, balanced blade thudding against the butcher block, I try to think of nothing at all. I simply move my knife over and over. I chop until the onions are minced.

"My goodness, Laine, that's fine enough." Mom leans over my shoulder. "One of these days you're going to cut yourself. Your eyes are so red, I don't know how you can see."

"I'm okay, Mom," I reply automatically. "Anyway, I'm done . . . and I have homework."

"Well, I appreciate your help. Looks like we're going to be busy tonight."

"Really?" I wipe my eyes on my apron and tug it over my head. "That's good. Holler if you need me."

"We'll be fine." Mom brushes a hand over my forehead. "Are you okay, Laine? You seem a little tired."

I give a dry laugh. "Physics and trigonometry, Mom."

My mother smiles and pulls me close. "Don't let the books get you down," she says warmly. "You're a natural scientist; I just know it."

"I hope so," I mutter as I head down the stairs to my mother's office.

Once I have the door to Mom's office open, I sit and play sudoku on her computer. The squares of numbers alternately frustrate and soothe me. When I hear someone coming, I blank the screen and open a book.

"What's up, Laine?"

I glance up, startled, as Sim bounds into the room. "I can't believe you're here" is the first thing out of my mouth. I wish I'd bitten my tongue.

"Got a makeup lab in physics," Sim says, and shrugs. "You kept your notes, right?"

Un*believable*. I glare at him, but he doesn't catch on. Did he only come here for that?

"Sim . . ." I make a disgusted noise and pick up my backpack. "Would it kill you to show up and take your *own* notes?"

"Probably," Sim replies.

"Wish it would," I mutter. I slap the notebook on the desk between us and go back to my sudoku.

"Thanks, Laine, I owe you one," Sim says, as he always does.

Actually, he owes me *two*, but who's counting? What's a little homework-sharing between friends? I glare at the computer screen, safely directing my irritation toward its blind, glassy eye. This is stupid. I know I shouldn't just let him treat me like this. I should say something. I should just open my mouth and say, *Simeon Keller, you can't have a party without inviting me*. Right. Like that would make me look cool and fun to hang out with and invite-able.

Never mind.

For once, Sim actually seems to be working . . . seriously. Every time he puts down his pen or turns a page, I expect for him to say something, something like, "Hey, Laine, I'm having this party." But he doesn't. He doesn't say a word.

A tangible silence crouches between us. I don't think I've ever seen him this quiet.

It's after five when Mom comes downstairs, and I think she's startled to find that I'm not alone. Sim and I haven't said a word to each other in over an hour.

"My goodness, this physics thing must be serious. Did you guys want any gazpacho? It's not a hot item on the service tonight, but it's tasty."

I shake my head. "Not yet."

Sim yawns. "Hey, Mrs. Seifert," he says. He glances at me, flicker-quick. "I'm done with your notes, Laine. Guess I'd better get going."

My mother immediately sits down on the corner of her desk. "Simeon. Wait a moment, if you would. I feel I owe you an apology—about the other day."

I shoot her a startled glance. Oh, Lord. *Not now, Mom.*

Simeon looks blank for a split second, and then that easy smile warms up his face. He pats my mother on the arm. "Mrs. Seifert, my mother always says that I trespass on your hospitality, so . . ."

Mom looks upset. "Simeon, you and Lainey have been *bosom buddies* for so long—"

"Mom!"

"—that we feel like you're practically family, but I just feel more comfortable with—"

"Mrs. Seifert. Really. There's nothing to apologize for. About. For which to apologize."

Sim's grinning now, and I suddenly just *itch* to slap him and remove that smug I-just-scored-here look from his face. He thinks he can always finesse himself out of anything, that he'll always have lackeys like me to take his notes for him and people like Mom totally fooled into believing he's the greatest thing since sliced bread. But I know how he really is. The words tumble out before I can stop them.

"Yeah, Mom, Sim's fine. He's feeling great. He's giving a little housewarming party at his new apartment this weekend, even."

Thunk. Bull's-eye. Sim shoots me a dirty look.

Mom looks floored. "A new apartment? Simeon, you have your own place?"

"Well, not *really*," Sim hedges, glaring at me. "It's just a little something I'm setting up, uh, since I'm turning eighteen pretty soon."

Pretty soon? Sim has another two months just like I do.

"Your parents are brave souls." Mom smiles uncertainly. "A place all your own. Wow. And you're going to pay your own bills and keep food on the table by yourself?"

"Well . . ." Sim stalls. "It's just, um, halfway my own place. Just sort of a trial thing."

Mom nods thoughtfully. "Well, I hope you make

your mom and dad proud." I make a derisive noise as my mother continues. "So I guess congratulations are in order. Is your party a potluck, or are you just having junk food? What did you want Lainey to bring?"

"Lainey's not invited," I say flatly. "So, Mom, who made the gazpacho? Is it an actual gazpacho with bread in it?"

My mother opens her mouth, then closes it, her deep brown eyes flicking to my face, then Simeon's. Sim's mouth tightens and he stands up and gathers his books.

"Lainey, walk me out." He picks up his backpack and heads for the door.

Not likely. I turn back toward my sudoku game. Sim comes back, grabs my arm, and drags me outside. My turncoat mother doesn't even bat an eye. Maybe she's remembering all the fights we had when we were little—"No girls allowed in my tree house!" "Stay away with your *cooties*!"—but this is a little different. Sim didn't used to be able to haul me around so easily.

We're toe to toe in the hallway outside my mother's office. "What?"

"Don't be . . . so . . . *feeble*," Sim snarls, practically inarticulate now that he's out of Mom's spotlight. "You know if you really want to come, you can come."

"'If' I really want to come? Whatever." I jerk away from him. This isn't what I want. What I want is a real invitation. What I *wanted* was not to have felt like an idiot all day, like the last person to know what was going on with my former best friend.

"Whatever, nothing. Show up if you want to."

"Why should I want to? Since when do I want to hang out with Carrigan?"

"Elaine!" Simeon throws up his hands. "I'm not hanging out with Carrigan. He invited himself and his friends, okay? I invited my friends. It's a party, and it's a free country. End of story. What's up with you?"

Yeah, Lainey, what's the matter with you? "Nothing, Sim. Just getting a good idea of where I stand in the 'friend' category lately."

"Ah, jeez, Laine. You know you don't party."

"Yeah. That's because I've been invited so many times. . . ."

Sim leans in, effectively silencing me with his louder voice. "Laine, look, I'm not going to apologize. I knew you wouldn't want to come, so I didn't say anything. Yeah, Carrigan's going to be there, and some of my other friends, and"—he lowers his voice—"you know you don't like parties when some of my other friends are invited. Okay?"

"Whatever, Sim." I don't think he could be more condescending.

"Elaine, what's your problem?"

I stare off at a point just above his shoulder, willing away tears of frustration. If this were even last year, we might have planned this party together. Even if I wasn't going, I would have known about everything. Now I want to say, "I was supposed to be your first guest," but I know he'll laugh at me or, worse, he'll be all condescending and "poor little Lainey." I'm feeling sorry for myself, stupid, and angry.

"Whatever." Sim's tired of waiting for an answer. "I'm done."

"Fine," I shoot back, and turn on my heel. Mom's talking to me before the reverberations of the slamming door have stopped.

"Lainey, what's going on?"

"Nothing. Sim's just being his usual stupid self."

Wisely, my mother leaves that alone. "Well, I meant it about the gazpacho," she begins.

"Thanks, Mom, but I'm not hungry."

I make a point of spending a lot of time on how I look the rest of the week, applying makeup for the first time in days and flat-ironing my hair instead of throwing it back in a ponytail. I wear a choker. I wear a skirt. Lip gloss. Mascara. War paint. Sim and I don't "see" each other in physics, but I'm pretty sure we both notice that I am trying to put a good face on the fact that he's having a party by proving to myself that I can have a good time without him. Every day at second period I chat with Cheryl and the other people around me, making an effort to be visible. I'm not making a scene, but I'm making a point: for a supposed-to-be best friend, it's wrong to issue a lame pseudo-invitation to a party; that's just the bottom line.

I get asked about five more times about the party, and by the end of the week, I feel like sticking a sign on my locker—**Loser: Not Invited.**

I know I'm jealous. And I know it's stupid. I just hate Sim's other . . . friends. He has people he hangs with for different hours of the day—jocks before school, stoners at lunch, preppies in the quad when he's cutting second, the "ride" freaks around their tricked-out cars in the parking lot . . . and me, off campus, after school, and only if he needs a favor. When I'm telling myself the truth, I wonder if we'd be friends if it weren't for the history behind us. When we were younger, I knew Sim liked me for my house—a safe place to hang, away from his mom and his family. Now that he has a place of his own and he and Carrigan are magically best buds and throwing parties, I guess that leaves me . . . out?

Sim doesn't come over for kindergarten the rest of the week, and I amaze myself by finishing all of my homework before it's anywhere near time for dinner. I spend so much time on my mother's computer that by Friday, I'm almost proficient at sudoku. Time hanging on my hands encourages me toward the restaurant kitchen, and I find myself fiddling with the idea for carrot macaroons. The recipe I come up with, taking ideas from other cookie recipes, is pretty basic, and after a while, I feel like it's time for a test run.

While the kitchen staff is prepping for the dinner rush, I grate a few carrots. Mom looks over my recipe and says it sounds good. When the first batch of golden cookies emerges from the oven, she comes over to sample.

"Mmm." She frowns. "How much coconut do these call for?"

"A half cup."

"You know, you could leave it out."

"I don't know. Would they still be macaroons?" We chew some more in silence as the kitchen rattles around us. "What do you think of the orange rind?"

"Good. You could use some extract if you wanted to define the flavor without adding another sugar source, like from a juice or something. Or you could try lime."

"That might really be good."

"You know, these are good enough to take to Sim's party."

What? I throttle down annoyance. "Try one of the ones with ginger."

"Lainey?"

"I guess you could put in almonds—kind of an amaretti thing?"

"Honey, I overheard, you know. He didn't not invite you. He just thought you wouldn't want to come. . . ."

"No almonds. But ginger. Yes?"

In the end, I decide to leave the orange rind and the fresh-grated ginger as optional add-ins so that the macaroons can pair with whatever ice cream or gelato is currently being featured. Pia comes by to taste and suggests pairing them with a pear granita, which is an Italian dessert ice that I love.

"This is a great idea to use for the holidays," Pia says proudly, reaching up to tap me on the shoulder. "This is just what we need—tasty ways to replace the old standards."

While she's talking, a big hand darts in between us to snatch a cookie. I turn and swat at it, laughing as the man attached to the hand holds the cookie out of my reach, which is easy for him to do. Stefan sniffs the cookie, looks at the color critically, and wrinkles his forehead.

"Well, it's pretty. What is it?"

"It's a cookie!" I poke him gently in the side. "Taste."

Stefan pops it into his mouth whole and chews thoughtfully. "Good," he mumbles. "Chewy, not too dense. The citrus is nice." He reaches for another.

"One of those is mine." Bethe, one of our sous-chefs, sets down her ladle and comes over with her hand outstretched. "I've been waiting for these."

Roy nips in and grabs one. Gene breaks his in half. He doesn't like sweets much.

"Hey, these are good." Ming, who ate Gene's other half, takes another. "I like the idea of an almond flavoring with these. Really nice, Laine."

When Gene comes back and asks where the other half of his cookie went, I can't keep back a crazy grin. This is what it would be like to have my own cooking show. *Seifert's Secrets*. Or maybe *The Lainey Files*. Yeah, I know I've got to really pay my dues before I get on TV and become the next Saint Julia, but this right now feels like the real thing. Everybody samples and chews and looks impressed, but then Mom glances at the clock and says, "Look at the time!" Pia starts shouting, and the kitchen starts jumping as the service for the night begins. I'm left alone with a plate of crumbs.

Here's the truth: I'm more comfortable behind the scenes in the kitchen than balancing a plate and eating neatly and making small talk about things that mean nothing to me. Even if I'd been invited, I really wouldn't belong at Simeon's party.

At home, I turn on the TV and fall asleep to the blue flicker, an old episode of *Yan Can Cook*.

LAINEY'S CARROT MACAROONS
(RECIPE IN PROGRESS!)

1/2 C. WHOLE WHEAT OR OAT FLOUR PLUS 1/2 C. OATS

1 1/2 C. GRATED RAW CARROTS, PACKED
 (SQUEEZED DRY - SEE NOTE BELOW)

1/2 C. WATER (MADE OUT OF THE WATER SQUEEZED OUT OF
 THE GRATED CARROTS!! DON'T WASTE THAT!)

1/3 C. REAL MAPLE SYRUP OR EQUIVALENT SUGAR SUBSTITUTE
 (DRY SUGAR SUBSTITUTE NEEDS MORE LIQUID SOMEWHERE -
 IF USING DRY, ADD 3 TBSP. WATER)

1/2 C. SHREDDED, UNSWEETENED COCONUT

1/2 TSP SALT

1 TSP. VANILLA EXTRACT

GRATED ORANGE RIND TO TASTE OR GINGER OPTIONAL

GRIND DRY (QUICK OR ROLLED - NO STEEL-CUT!) OATS TO
MAKE A COARSE FLOUR. (COULD USE OAT FLOUR BUT ROUGH
GROUND GIVES MORE BODY.) ADD 1/2 C. WHEAT FLOUR.
MIX WELL ALL INGREDIENTS. LET SIT 10 MINUTES
(OR MORE IF YOU HAVE TIME).

FIRMLY PACK DOUGH INTO A TBSP. THEN DROP ON AN
OILED BAKING SHEET. BAKE AT 325°F FOR 30
MINUTES.

* * MOM THINKS THE COCONUT CAN BE DROPPED

* * PIA SAYS TO SERVE WITH A GRANITA — CAN
BE MADE SWEETER. . . .

8

By Monday, I have my head on straight. After hanging out at the restaurant all weekend, I realize that I know where my life is going, and I don't need people like Simeon Keller to succeed. It's just that simple. I vow to act like nothing is going on, like I did on Friday, and make a point of bringing fresh ginger macaroons to Vocal Jazz. I am awake enough not to need coffee and to sing along with Manhattan Transfer's "A-Tisket, A-Tasket." Ms. Dunston is pleased. Ben is not.

"Show-off." Ben grins, then cracks a mighty yawn.

I shrug. "I'm just awake for once."

"I shouldn't have gone out this weekend," Ben mumbles, like I've asked. "I'm still totally wiped."

Still? I hesitate, then delicately fish for information. "Good party, huh?"

Ben confirms my guess while knuckling his eyes.

"Yeah, at Sim Keller's. I didn't go Friday, but I heard some guys from the junior college brought a keg on Saturday, so a bunch of us went. Heard the cops came after I left."

I nod, but inside, I roll my eyes. The cops. *Please*. That's the epitaph every party gets—the cops came, broke up the action, everyone went home. The cops probably didn't show, but it's the mark of a successful high school party that the rumor says they did.

It's just as well that I didn't go. A keg? *See, Mom*, I think. Lainey and her little cookies would have been way out of their league.

Party-boy Sim isn't at school Monday, but Carrigan is, doing his usual "you're invisible" glance that slides over me. There's nothing unusual in that at all, but I do hear some kind of buzz going on about a couple of kids being in trouble, including Christopher Haines, not that I believe that, even if he did miss Vocal Jazz this morning.

Friday, Cheryl leans across the aisle before the warning bell and asks how Sim is doing. I'm annoyed by the question and doubly annoyed because I'm wondering the same thing. We have a physics test on Monday that accounts for twenty-five percent of our grade, and our tutorial was last night. I'm pretty sure Sim's going to show soon enough, trying to butter me up for my physics notes. Fat chance.

I shrug and root around in my backpack for a pen. "Sim? Beats me. We don't exactly talk these days."

"Oh." Cheryl sounds subdued.

I glance up, frowning. "What's up?"

Cheryl half shrugs. "Oh, you know, the party. After the cops came and busted everybody for the keg and the smoke and stuff, he bailed. I heard he got picked up, but I guess they sprung him since he didn't test positive for anything. Then his dad threw a fit, and I guess they had it out, and now nobody can find him."

"What?" My hand comes up to my mouth automatically as my brain processes three thoughts at once—Ben was serious, the cops were real, Sim is— "No way! I—" The second bell rings, and I break off abruptly. Mr. Wilcox is standing at the front of the room, ready to begin our chapter review. I have so many questions, but there's only time for one.

I drop my voice and lean across the aisle. "You were there?"

Cheryl nods. "For a while," she admits.

Physics is a blur, and I stare at our video in European history without seeing much of it. I'm not hungry by fourth period, so I'm on my way to the library when I see that the door to the English room is open. I knock on the frame.

"Mrs. Spaulding?" The words are coming out of my mouth meekly.

The cramps excuse rarely works with teachers, and Mrs. Spaulding probably doesn't really believe me, but I don't care. I promise her faithfully that I will finish the reading and turn in an extra assignment tomorrow, then I'm out of there.

I, Lainey Seifert, am cutting class!

I don't know where I'm going or what I'm going to do, but I want to find Simeon. I hitch my backpack onto my shoulder and dig my cell out of the front pocket. I hardly use it, but along with Mom's, Sim's number is one of the few I have programmed in. I push the speed dial button and listen to it ring. *Pick up,* I think, but of course he doesn't. I nervously leave a message.

"Sim . . . it's me. I just . . . heard." I'm breathless and talking too fast. I slow down, take a deep breath. "I just wanted you to know I'm sorry. . . . I . . . I guess you were right." I take another deep breath. "About the party." My voice gets wobbly. "Sorry, Sim."

I hang up before I say anything worse.

It's a longer walk, but avoiding First Street, where Mom might see me, is best, since even I can't explain what I'm doing or where I'm going. All the way home I remember every single time Sim's said he's going to "just go" or "disappear" and I feel myself starting to worry. I lie down on my bed and try to do my reading for English lit, but eventually I lay aside my book and stare at the ceiling.

Sim had parties all weekend, and now he's been . . .
nowhere—for a week. I close my eyes. There is so much
I have said that I wish I could take back.

When the telephone rings, I know it's Mom.

"Hey, Laineybelle," she says cheerfully. "Good, you're
home. Simeon isn't over, is he?"

My throat tightens. "Sim? No."

"You're not getting another cold, are you?"

"No," I say clearly. "What about Sim?"

"His mother phoned this morning," Mom says.
"You'd already left for school. . . . She wanted to know if
he'd been around this weekend. Did you two make up?"

"No." The word holds a wealth of information.

"Why don't you come down to the restaurant,
honey?" The sadness in my voice wakes an answering
sympathy in my mother's.

"I'm okay, Mom. I'm just going to finish up my reading and cook something."

"You sure, Laine?"

"Really, Mom, I'm fine." I force brightness into my
tone, and after repeated assurances, she hangs up.

I put down the phone and flip on my computer, then
turn it off. No e-mail. I turn on the TV and flip channels.
I can't settle, and there's only one thing in my life that
lets me unwind.

I turn on some lights and go downstairs. Determined

to lighten the mood, I turn on classical music, Camille Saint-Saëns and his romantic violins, and pull out a pot of Mom's leftover mushroom soup. When I have my cooking show, I think I'll use classical music for the show's theme, like Jeff Smith from the old episodes of *The Frugal Gourmet* before it went off the air. I can never hear that piece from Vivaldi's *Four Seasons* without remembering that show.

I open the pot of soup and sniff. Even cold it smells good. Much of what is in the fridge is from La Salle, but Mom actually made this mushroom soup herself, starting out with dehydrated mushrooms, onions, and white wine. I decide to make a matzo ball soup.

"To begin our stock, let's heat up the soup and add some leeks and four stalks of celery to revive the taste. While it is simmering, we'll mix up a cup of matzo meal with four eggs, a half teaspoon of plain club soda, finely chopped parsley, coarse ground black pepper, and a pinch of salt," I inform my imaginary studio audience. I clear my throat. My studio voice needs work.

I mix up the matzo, place the sticky dough into the fridge, and go back to the soup. I add carrots and then hunt through the root cellar for something else. Our root cellar is just a wooden chest on the pantry floor, filled with clean sand, where Mom stores root veggies in the winter. There's not much in there now, but I find a rutabaga and a parsnip. I chop the rutabaga and add it to the soup, setting aside the strong-tasting parsnip for further study; Mom's constantly filling our root cellar with new and strange foods, and there's bound to be something good to do with this one.

I'm grating zucchini for the latkes, humming to the *Carnival of the Animals* and getting ready to talk to my audience about the merits of trying new flavors, when I hear the front door. Mom hasn't popped in to check on me in a long time. I must've sounded depressed on the phone. I'm feeling much better now. Cooking is such a beautiful distraction. I think when I have my cooking show, I'm going to have Mom drop by and do a show just on that.

"Hey, Mom? Do you think parsnips and carrots would work for latkes like the zucchini and summer squash? I think I might try . . ." I jerk, zucchini flying from nervous fingers.

"You rang?" Sim stands in the living room, holding his cell, a half smirk on his face.

"What are you doing here?!"

Sim's eyes are muddy dark, and his pupils are huge. He is pale and dusty, like he slept outside last night. He runs a hand through his hair and gives me a strained smile. "Sorry to scare you. I used my key."

"Your key?!" My brain's still on "cooking show." I can't process Sim being here.

Sim licks his lips nervously. "Yeah. Do you think you could—?"

"Wait, are you—?" Our sentences collide. I start again. "Sim, where have you been? Did you know your mom called here? And where'd you get a key?"

He holds out a key on a chain around his neck: our house key. "Seventh grade, remember? I watered the plants?"

"You made a *copy*?"

Sim sighs. "Laine, forget the key for a second, willya? I'm kind of stuck. I need a place to . . ." Simeon trails off, shrugs, and then smiles his usual smile. It looks more like a grimace.

"Sim, what's going on?"

"Ah, just the usual crap." Sim smiles again, but he can't look at me.

"Oh, Sim . . ." Impulsively, I cross the room and awkwardly put my arms around him. He grips me like he's going to break my ribs. He has been outside for a while; I can feel it in the cold in his clothes. He smells like sour sweat, smoke, and other things that I can't quite name, like he hasn't changed clothes since the party.

"You can hang out," I tell his collar. "I'm making soup, but you can have whatever. And you can sleep or talk, and Mom won't be home for a while, but I'll get you everything you need, and it'll be okay. Okay?"

I'm listening to Simeon's silence, my throat clogging

as my words wind down. He doesn't make any noise as he holds on to me. No noise at all. And I fall silent in the face of such misery.

"Why," Simeon croaks finally, "does everything always turn to crap?"

Man, what do I say to that?

Even as my heart is constricted in sympathy, I can feel myself wanting to run around the room screaming, "He's back! He's back!"

Simeon gives a huge sigh and leans away from me. "Um, Laine? Do you mind if I use your shower?"

My *shower*? "Um . . . okay. No problem. Do you want to wash your clothes? You can wear some of my old sweats. . . ."

Sim nods. "Thanks. I . . . uh, haven't been home long enough to unpack."

"Why not? Is—?"

"*Laine.*" He sounds almost angry, and I back off. Things like, "Is everything okay?" and "Are the police looking for you?" are obviously not things someone cool would say. Instead, I show Sim our washer and dryer upstairs, dig out a pair of old sweats, comfort clothes from four sizes ago, and more of Mom's wool socks, and leave Sim clean towels. I go back downstairs and check on my soup, and because I can't think of anything else to do, I keep grating squash. That's what chefs do, I guess, when they need to. People have to eat.

*   *   *

By the time the latkes are done, I've chopped up a fresh apple, zapped it in the microwave until it's very soft, and added it to the warm applesauce and Chinese five-spice mixture I've made. I hesitate as I put it on the table; Sim might not like spicy applesauce. My stomach is cowering behind my ribs, and I hate how nervous I am. This is just Sim, my ex–best friend, the guy who totally blows me off unless he needs my physics notes. This is just food, just dinner, just something to eat. This isn't a cooking show, there are no lights and no studio audience, and there are no expectations for a gourmet meal, so why do I feel like this?

My hand shakes as I put out a bowl of plain yogurt to go with the latkes.

I turn down the mushroom soup, strain out the bits until I have a broth, and set aside the limp vegetables. The broth comes to a boil, and I roll the matzo dough, cold and stiff, into golf-ball-sized balls and drop them into the soup. The matzo balls sink like the sticky stones they are and finally rise, signaling their doneness.

Simeon still hasn't come downstairs.

I run my hands under the tap and dry them on a dish towel. I wonder nervously if Sim's okay, and I want to yell to him, like I would in times past, that dinner's ready, but the sound of his silence is strangling me. This is not a night for yelling and clomping up and down.

Finally, I go to the stairwell and suck in my breath,

my heart banging against my ribs. Sim is sitting hunched over on the bottom stair.

"Sorry," he mutters as I gasp and clutch my chest. "Didn't mean to scare you."

He looks both better and worse. His hair is damp and curling back from his face, but his eyes look like empty, pink-rimmed holes in his tired face.

"What are you doing down there?"

"Nothing. Didn't want to interrupt. Did you know you kind of hum when you cook?"

My face twitches, my expression confused between a smile and a roll of my eyes. "Do you want to eat right here, or . . . ?"

Sim gives me a look with a ghost of his old smile. "I still know where the table is."

"Well, then, why didn't you come to the table instead of camping out on the stairs?"

Simeon swallows, his smile fading. "I was thinking I should go," he says, and I give a short laugh.

"Before dinner? Be serious, Sim. Let's eat."

VIV'S VEGGIE LATKES

2 C. GRATED YELLOW SQUASH AND/OR ZUCCHINI
1/2 C. GRATED ONION
2 EGGS (OR 4 EGG WHITES, BEATEN)
1/2 TSP. DASH OF SALT AND GROUND PEPPER, OR CHOPPED
   SAGE, OR SUMMER SAVORY, OR WHATEVER
OLIVE OIL SPRAYED ON A NONSTICK PAN

SQUEEZE EXCESS WATER FROM SQUASH
* TOO MUCH LIQUID, THE LATKES FALL APART!

IN A LARGE BOWL, COMBINE ALL INGREDIENTS, THEN HEAT A
LARGE NON-STICK GRIDDLE OVER HIGH HEAT; IT WILL BE HOT
ENOUGH WHEN A DROP OF WATER SIZZLES WHEN DROPPED
ON SURFACE. CAREFULLY DROP 1 HEAPING TBSP. OF LATKE BATTER
ONTO THE HOT GRIDDLE AND FLATTEN WITH A SPATULA TO FORM
PANCAKE SHAPE. (DON'T PUT TOO MANY — DON'T CROWD THEM.)
COOK FOR A COUPLE MINUTES ON EACH SIDE OR UNTIL
GOLDEN BROWN. REPEAT UNTIL NO BATTER REMAINS.

TO ADD NEW FLAVOR, ADD FRESH ROSEMARY TO ZUCCHINI,
OR OREGANO AND FRESH PARSLEY TO ~~SUMMER~~ YELLOW SQUASH.

* * TRY PLAIN YOGURT INSTEAD OF SOUR CREAM.

FLAVOR YOGURT WITH DILL?

* * ADD CUMIN TO BOTH - ABOUT 1/4 TSP. - GOOD FLAVOR.

* * NOTE * * TRY THIS WITH CARROTS?

* SQUASH WATERY IF NOT WELL DRAINED - ADD 2 TBSP.

HERBED BREADCRUMBS TO SOP LIQUIDS?

9

"Are the latkes okay?"

Sim nods, spooning in another bite of soup. "They're fine."

I can barely taste my food, but Sim's eating enough for both of us. I'm uncomfortable in the silence at my own table. I feel like I opened up my front door and let in some kind of untamed animal, and it's holding me at bay at my end of the room.

Of course, I didn't let him in. That still bothers me a little.

Too tightly wound to sit anymore, I push back from the table, heading into the living room to light a fire. The phone rings as I'm stacking up kindling, and Sim doesn't look like he's miles away anymore. "Don't pick up." The tightness to his jaw makes the hair stand up on my arms.

"What?" I freeze and stare at him.

"Don't pick up. I know who it is."

I'm baffled. "So do I. It's my mom. She calls me every night at this time."

"It might not be."

"You can check the caller ID."

The phone is on its third ring. If I don't pick up and it is Mom . . . I ignore his glare and stretch for the cordless phone.

"Hi, Lainey." Mom's voice sounds anxious. "Are you feeling better? You were sounding a little depressed earlier."

"I'm fine, Mom. I just made some soup, and I'm going to watch a movie." I look at Simeon with exaggeratedly wide eyes, mouthing, *See?*

"Oh, good." Mom sounds relieved. "I was going to pop by and make sure you were doing okay . . . I still can. Want me to bring you something?"

"No—no, Mom, I'm okay. I made latkes too, so I'm not doing any dessert."

"You sure? Pia's having a good night with coconut torte. If you find Sim, you could—"

Yikes. "N-no, thanks, Mom. I'm good, really."

"Well, okay. I better get back—big crowd tonight." I can hear the pride and the nervousness in my mother's voice.

"That's great! Well, break a chicken leg or something."

"Ha! Vegetarian humor. Enjoy your movie, honey. You do sound better."

Mom says something else nice, then I hang up the phone and finish piling wood into the fireplace.

"Your mom calls you every night?"

I blink. Shrug. "Yeah." I don't bother telling him she also calls me when she knows I'll be home from school. Mom is always calling to check up on me. But she is very cool about it. Mostly. When it isn't totally annoying. I shrug again.

Sim relaxes a little and watches me make the fire, still sitting at the table, fiddling with his soup spoon. I offer him more soup, but he shakes his head. He picks a piece off the last latke and nibbles on it, his face expressionless.

"You're really quiet," I say finally.

He shrugs and watches the flames.

I quirk my eyebrows, but nothing else seems forthcoming, so I clear the table, put on the kettle for hot chocolate, and try to figure out if I should make dessert. If we watch a movie, snacks might come in handy, so I pull out four Fuji apples from the fruit basket and dig out the apple corer. I think about chopping them up to make an apple crisp, but I decide against it and put back all but two of the biggest apples for baking.

I glance over my shoulder again at the statue at my

table. How long do you have to be friends with someone before you're allowed to ask about the details of their life? Is that some girlfriend privilege I haven't been given? I'm dying to ask him what's going on . . . but should I?

"Laine, I need to tell you something," Sim says, and I twitch guiltily.

"Hmm?"

The corer has a spot on it. I run it under the tap and pick at it. There are no clean dish towels within reach, so I open the drawer and pull out a fresh one. I dry the corer and then wash off the apples for good measure. For some reason, I don't want to hear what Sim has to say.

"Laine, what are you messing with?"

"Nothing." I turn off the water and face him, arms crossed. "What?"

"You know, my therapist would say that you're looking very *closed* right now," Sim says suddenly. Steepling his fingers in front of his face and narrowing his eyes, Simeon does his Freud imitation. "Da ist sometink troubling you, Fräulein?"

I roll my eyes. "Sim . . ."

He sighs. "Okay. I need to ask a favor."

Simeon's "favors" in the past have usually been limited to physics notes in those bursts of industry where he actually acts like he has to, I don't know, turn in assignments to graduate. I have a bad feeling that this isn't about school.

"Okay, a favor." I turn a little away from him, grab the corer, and sink it with a satisfying thunk into an apple. I may as well keep going on dessert.

I core the second apple before I realize that Sim isn't going to keep talking until I'm looking at him. Frowning, I twist around and stare exaggeratedly. "Okay, Sim. I'm *listening*. The favor. So, *ask*."

He lifts his chin. No smile. "I'm going to disappear."

I put down the apple, work on clearing the seeds and pith from the corer. I try to keep my voice level to combat the jump my stomach just took. "Disappear? Your family hire the Mafia or something?" Lame joke.

"Lainey . . . I'm . . . I need to leave. I need you to help me."

I stop and frown at him, the apple bits sticky in my hands. I halfway expect some continuation of Sim's usual antic, some kind of gangster line like, "Things are too hot for me here, sister. I'm gonna blow this joint." But . . . nothing.

I've been biting my tongue all evening, effectively putting a cork into any concern or questions. Now they come pouring out.

"Leave? Sim, is . . . Did you . . . ?" I take a deep breath. "Simeon, what happened? I hear from Cheryl Fisk that you got picked up for possession or something and you're going to rehab? Is—"

"Lainey . . . ," Simeon interrupts impatiently. "Look. Don't . . ." He gestures wordlessly, as if trying to pull out the words from where they hid. "I don't want to go into it, okay? I'm not some kind of junkie, the police are not looking for me, and no, I'm not going to rehab. No drama, all right? I'm just leaving. I said one day I would. I . . . Everything just got too messed up."

"Sim—"

"Elaine, I just wanted to say goodbye is all. You called; I thought about it; I thought I'd come by. I'm not coming back."

The words just thud into my brain. I stand and stare. "Wha—"

"*Laine*," Simeon sighs, and I close my mouth.

There are so many questions I want to ask. Why won't he let me ask them?

The apples are turning brown. I finish them, then methodically gather the bits of apple core, put them into the counter composting bin, and rinse my hands. I set the apples in their identical little glass bowls and am halfway to filling them with cardamom and granola before Simeon speaks again.

"I finally figured it out," he continues, as if he's just thought of this. "My parents are crazy, and they're making

126

me crazy, and it's them that's making my life such crap. I can't live like this, so I'm not going to. It's not like they don't want me to go."

"So, you're just . . . going." I'm having a hard time making sense of the thoughts in my head. The *What about me?* that I keep hearing wailing up from my heart I smother in favor of common sense, the voice in my head. This is Simeon. There is no "me" in the equation. There hasn't ever been, and I know it, so why can't I get that through my head?

"What—" I clear my throat, try again. "So, are you going to, like, run away from home?" It's easier to camouflage my feelings in sarcasm, to hide my nerves in action, in the movement of my thumbs tamping the filling down in the empty heart of the apple.

"I'm not 'running away,' Laine," Sim says, his voice putting a mocking emphasis on the words. "I did that when I was, like, seven."

"No, you were ten," I remember suddenly. "We read *My Side of the Mountain* in Mr. Leith's class, and the next week you walked all the way to San Rosado Park with a suitcase and stayed under a tree all day."

Sim's smile is faint. "Elaine, this is just a *bit* different."

I shrug. "Not that much."

"Well, it is," Sim replies tightly. "I'm sick of being played, Laine. There's nothing for me here anymore;

there's no reason to stay." He sighs. "I need to get out of California, get to where I have a little more room to live. Everybody breathes down your neck around here."

I don't know what to say, but it doesn't really matter. Just talking about leaving seems to make Sim's mood elevate; suddenly he is animated, his hands moving to punctuate his words.

"If it were closer to the season, I'd head up to Alaska and hire on to a fishing boat," he begins, standing and coming to lean on the counter next to me. He hitches a hip up against the butcher-block corner and grins. "It's early for that; they only hire for the big boats in the summer, but now's the time to start networking, applying for the jobs, and getting the lay of the land. I can also take a cruise ship job if working commercial fishing doesn't pan out. There's a lot of seasonal work in Alaska if you're willing to hustle."

I concentrate on preheating the oven, dusting cinnamon over the apples, and washing my hands. Next I will concentrate on wiping down the counter, putting away my ingredients, and turning off the CD. By then, maybe I'll figure out something to say.

Sim is still talking. "There's just a lot of stuff I can do, you know? It came to me—just like that—I'm not really stuck. There's no one keeping me here. There's no one holding a gun to my head going, 'Live here or else.' I mean, seriously—I can always bail. . . . Lainey? Are you even listening to me?"

"Sorry. I'm listening. I just . . ." I shrug helplessly, aware that's been my only response for some time. It's the best I can do. If I say anything at all right now, I'm afraid it will be, "How can you just ditch me?" or something like, "What do you mean, there's no one keeping you here?" or, "Don't you care about me at all?" I keep my mouth shut, bite my tongue, keep my hands busy.

Sim looks at me for a moment and narrows his eyes. For a disquieting moment, I wonder what it is he sees, exactly. Then his face clears and he nods.

"I get it. You're waiting for the favor."

Favor? And then I remember. "Yeah." I shrug and cross my arms in front of me. "What's the favor?"

Simeon shoves his hands in his pockets and blows out a sharp sigh. "Okay, here's the thing. I need to borrow some money," he says shortly. "The down on the apartment left me a little short for leaving town. Since my father's figuring out a way to break the lease, I think they're going to give it back, but . . . it won't be for a while, and I don't plan to be around to collect. I'll send you the money from the road first thing, and I know I'll find a job—the guys at Soy already told me they'd give me references. I just need a couple hundred bucks." Simeon stops, then adds unnecessarily, "I know your grandma Muriel always sent you something, and you still have it because you hardly ever do anything. . . ."

"Sim! Jeez!"

"Well, you don't, and it'll just be a loan, I swear." He rakes his fingers through his hair, looking away. His voice is harsh. "I've never asked you for anything like this, Laine. This is important."

I face him, my hands empty of little tasks to occupy them. I need to say this fast before I lose my nerve. "Simeon, I'd loan you any amount of money, you know that, and it's because I . . . love you, and not just because I have it and 'don't do anything with it,' so don't be a total jackass about it if you can help it. I just wish . . ."

I look at the floor, shove my hands in my pockets, look back at Simeon. "You didn't . . . I mean, can't you . . . isn't there anything . . ." I gulp and cross my arms. "Sim, are you sure you have to go?"

The words *Don't go, I'll miss you* are lodged against my vocal cords.

Sim shakes his head impatiently. "You don't get it, do you? See, you've got this great house, this great mom, this safe little Lainey world that's all yours, and everything you want. I have to fight just to get by, and everybody's always on me. I can't live like that." His voice is hoarse, raw with emotion. "I have to do this, Elaine. I don't have a soft place to land when everything goes to hell. I have to leave in order to have a *life*." His voice cracks on the last word, and he paces away from me, twisting his ring, his head tilted forward to let his hair hide his face.

"Sim. I didn't mean . . ."

I never mean to be insensitive, but Sim makes me sound like I'm completely clueless, self-absorbed, and spoiled. Sure, I've never thought of myself as particularly lucky, but truthfully, only because I never think of it at all. I had a father once who loved me and two grandmothers, one of whom is still alive to dote on me. I have Mom. We have each other. But even though he has an entire family, what does Sim really have?

I swallow. "Sim. You know you're my best friend. I'll help you all I can."

"It'll be a *loan*, Lainey. I promise. I promise."

"How much . . . ?"

Sim sighs. "Five hundred, but I'll take whatever."

Five hundred dollars. My stomach clenches. That kind of money will wipe out almost my entire account.

"Okay." I breathe. "Have you called for a bus reservation?"

Sim shakes his head. "It's only in person, if you pay cash."

"So . . ." I am cautious about asking too much.

"So, I'm not going to take the bus. It'll stretch the

131

money further if I hitch. I know a guy in Seattle who knows a guy who runs an RV place. I can camp until I get on my feet."

"Sim . . . hitching. That's a really bad idea."

"Do you think I don't *know that*?" Sim sounds hostile, frustrated. "Laine . . ."

I sigh. "Can you go home and get your camping stuff?"

Sim shrugs. "There's an army surplus store up there. I can rough it."

"Pia has a chef friend who backpacks in the Pacific Northwest and picks mushrooms. . . . She stays at hostels."

Sim shrugs indifferently. "It doesn't matter where I stay."

"Well, at least we can look online."

Upstairs I type in some search words. I breathe a sigh of relief when I find one of the places Pia talked about. The Sagehill Hostel has dorm rooms, private rooms, and a Laundromat, making it a perfect place to wait out the weather. Better still, they have a work-a-week deal where he would pay less in return for doing office jobs or cleaning.

"That sounds better than camping." I turn to Sim wearily. "I just wish you weren't hitching."

Sim throws up his hands. "What else am I going to

do? My dad's already told me if I even borrow the car, he's going to have me up on charges of grand theft."

I flinch. "Sorry . . ."

Simeon sighs. "Sorry. I'm sorry. I don't mean to yell. Just . . . don't . . ." He rubs a hand over his face.

I leave Simeon upstairs and pick up my jacket on the way out the front door. I need a break, and now seems as good a time as any to go to a cash machine. I wish Simeon weren't so angry and frustrated. I wish I didn't feel like arguing with everything he says. I know I'm asking too many questions. I know I'm getting on his nerves. I know, I know, I *know*. But I don't know how to stop. This is huge. This is major. The money, Sim leaving—everything. I don't know how to handle any of this.

It's cold and windy out, and I wish I didn't have to walk downtown on such a blustery night. I feel a cold, heavy dread in my stomach. I've never held that much cash in my life. What if someone sees me? What if I get robbed on the way home?

Stop being stupid, Lainey.

I put in my card and quickly type out my PIN code.

The machine hums and gives me a polite refusal. I can't withdraw that amount from my account without going inside the bank during business hours, and it's after five on a Friday. Sim needs this money right now, but there's nothing I can do. Or . . .

Biting my bottom lip, I glance at Mom's checking account. Plenty of money is there, more than enough to cover what Simeon needs. When I get home, I can just transfer the amount from my savings into her checking account online. I have my mother's password; I can do it.

I've shared Mom's account since I was about thirteen. I've never used it without telling her. I am going to pay her back, but it feels too much like lying to use her account and not be able to tell her that I did it or why. Lying to my mom is the one thing that I just don't do; it's Mom's one deal breaker. Throughout my whole life, the only times I've ever gotten into real trouble have been when I've lied. And it seems like everything I've ever lied to her about has had to do with Sim, from broken toys and stolen cookies to Halloween pranks and crank phone calls. But it was never anything this serious.

But thinking about our shared past gives me the courage I need. This is Sim. I've known him forever. I take a deep breath and push the buttons to make my withdrawal. The machine spits back my card, and the little window goes up on $500, Cash.

I shove the roll of cash into my pocket, then pull it out again and stick it under my shirt. I cross my arms and cross the street briskly, heading home. I resist the urge to run.

The minute I walk in the front door, I know I'm in trouble. I hadn't even glanced into the garage to see if her car was there, but when I open the front door, it's like a jolt to my stomach. I can smell her—a faint mix of shallots and garlic overlaid lightly with herbs.

"Mom?"

"Elaine Seifert! What were you doing out walking in the dark?"

"I just took a walk," I say defensively. I cross to the oven and turn it off, shoving my unbaked apples into the fridge, hoping my mother doesn't notice. "I was coming right back."

My mother studies me. "Lainey, sometimes . . ." She shakes her head.

"What?" I lean against the table and cross my arms. "Sometimes what?"

My mother shakes her head again. "I'm not going to get into it with you right now. I'm just here to change my shoes." Mom turns and starts climbing the stairs. "Do you want to come back to the restaurant with me?"

"No, I'm fine." I jog along behind her nervously. "I'm going to maybe watch a movie, maybe make some apples, and definitely go to bed." Where is Sim? I notice that my bedroom door is half open.

"Hmm," my mother says noncommittally, no longer listening as she walks down the hall. She opens her closet door and pulls out a pair of clogs with a cork insole. "Can you believe my strap broke?" My mother frowns and slides into the new shoes. "I should have gotten the rubber ones Pia got."

"Pia's are ugly."

Mom smiles. "I know." Closing the closet, she leans into the mirror, scrutinizing her chef's jacket for spots, pecks me on the cheek, then brushes past me out the door and down the stairs. "Stay inside, okay? And don't stay up too late," she calls over her shoulder.

"Mom, it's the weekend. What's too late on a weekend?"

My mother gives a theatrical sigh, and then she's gone.

I stand at the top of the stairs and breathe in relief. The moment I hear the lobby door close, I sprint for my room and throw open the door.

"She's—"

The room is empty.

I stop, stunned, my mouth open. I walk around the side of the bed.

"Sim?"

Silence.

Worried now, I race through the house. The guest room, the closet, downstairs in the pantry, the coat closet, none of these give me any clues. Maybe he left right after I did. Maybe he had something else to do.

Confused, I sit down on my bed and pull the money out from under my shirt. I count it, then put it into my sock drawer. I pick up the telephone.

"Sim"—I leave the message on his cell—"um . . . I'm home, and Mom's gone, so . . . you can come back, okay?"

It's eight-thirty before I realize that I'm sitting alone in my house, watching the clock like I've been stood up for a date or something. Sim's still not back, and now I'm torn between worry and anger. Could something have happened to him? Could he have left already? I think of how aggravated he was when I went to the bank. Was that our goodbye?

I'm up like a shot when the phone rings, but it's just Mom again, asking if I'll e-mail a file to her office computer. Online, I go into our bank site and transfer funds from my savings to her checking. It will be time-stamped, but . . . I cross my fingers. Maybe Mom won't notice.

At eleven-fifteen, I pull back my hair and put on my flannel nightshirt, resigned. He's left without the money, and he's not coming back. I get into bed and turn out the lights so I won't have to see myself reflected in the windows anymore, pacing back and forth. I swallow the rock in my throat and lie staring into the darkness. I refuse to cry.

I'm still awake when Mom comes, after midnight. She opens my bedroom door a crack like she always does, and I lie still and breathe evenly as she watches me by the glow of the night-light. I hear her door closing, and soon her light goes out, and the house is utterly silent. I stare at the ceiling wondering if this has all been a joke. Has Mom noticed the money?

"Laine."

A hand is on my shoulder. I turn over and mumble something. It's too early.

"Laine. Don't freak, okay? Move over."

BASIC BAKED APPLES

2 TSP. BUTTER

PLANE-GRATED FRESH CINNAMON, FENNEL SEEDS, AND CLOVES
(CARDAMOM IS A WINNER. STAR ANISE?)

1/3 C. QUICK-COOKED OATS, OR INSTANT OATMEAL.
(SUBSTITUTING CRUSHED DRY CEREAL WORKS TOO.)

2 TBSP. RAW SUGAR PLUS 1 TSP. HONEY OR 1 HEAPING
    TBSP., PLUS 1 TSP. DARK BROWN SUGAR

2. FUJI APPLES

PREHEAT OVEN TO 350°F

MIX TOGETHER BUTTER, SPICES, OATS, AND 2 TBSP. SUGAR.
USING AN APPLE CORER, BORE OUT THE CENTER OF YOUR
FUJI APPLE, AND PACK SUGAR MIXTURE INSIDE. (MAYBE ADD
RAISINS OR 2 TBSP. CHOPPED DATES FOR VARIETY.)
WRAP IN FOIL, AND BAKE FOR ABOUT 40 MINUTES.
APPLES SHOULD BE SOMEWHAT FIRM BUT SOFT AND FRAGRANT.
TOP WITH DRIZZLE OF HONEY OR BROWN SUGAR.
SERVE WITH ICE CREAM AND A SPRINKLING OF
CHOPPED NUTS OR WHIPPED CREAM AND POWDERED SUGAR.

* * USE GRANNY SMITH FOR A MORE TART AND JUICY
FLAVOR, AND ADD 1/3 TSP. LIME ZEST. CUT SUGAR
TO SAVE CALORIES. SUGAR IS 50 CALORIES PER TBSP. —
AND IF THE APPLE'S RIPE, IT'S SWEET ENOUGH.

* * USE FENNEL SPARINGLY — CAN BE TOO STRONG.

* * SAINT JULIA MADE ~~STEAMED~~ STEAMED ~~BAKED~~ APPLES
— FIND RECIPE IN MOM'S BOOK.

10

The covers shift. Suddenly I'm cold, wide awake, and panicking.

"Sim?!" My heart trip-hammers, and my mouth goes dry. *He's getting into bed?!*

"Shh! Don't freak, Laine." He's barely whispering.

"What are you *doing*? What time is it?"

"It's two-ish. Sorry to barge in on you, but I'm just going to get warmed up, okay?"

Okay? I reach for the lamp, and Sim touches my arm. His hand is cold.

"No lights, Lainey. Relax."

I let my hand drop, feeling sweat prickle beneath my arms as Sim slides under the covers. I sit stiffly as he scootches down, imagining the screaming if my mother were to come in right now. His shirt smells like incense and smoke.

"It's freezing out there!" Sim's teeth are chattering.

I have a death grip on my pillow. "Where'd you go?"

"Just around. I got my clothes, and I was in the bathroom changing when your mom came in. Good thing you've got a big window. I chucked everything in the tub and climbed down the fire escape." He chuckles.

I clutch the pillow closer to my chest. "I didn't know where you were."

"Sorry." I feel Sim shrug. "I didn't know how long she'd be, so I made some phone calls, found some people to hang out with, you know."

I know. I can smell the smoke in his hair, and if I turned on the lights, his eyes would probably be red. I picture the look on my mother's face if she saw him and shiver.

"Are you cold? Jeez, Laine, I'm sorry. Here. Get under the covers."

"I'm okay," I say faintly, feeling dizzy.

Sim is laughing. "Laine, are you seriously scared of me here?"

I feel my face flaming. "No! I just . . ."

"Lie *down*, will you? I'm completely too wasted to jump you right now." Sim snickers.

"Shut up." I smack him on the top of the head and lie down, feeling conscious of how much space my body takes, where his ends and mine begins.

"Much better," Sim says, and puts his head on my shoulder. "Do you tell bedtime stories?"

"Shut *up*, Sim." But I'm smiling.

"I really appreciate this, Laine." Air tickles my ear. "I swear I'm leaving tomorrow."

I shrug stiffly, as if I don't care, but my senses are overwhelmed, feeling Simeon's hair on my neck, the heat of his shoulder pressing against my arm. He doesn't seem to need my reply to keep on talking.

"Need to get some sleep now. I've got a ride at seven-ish or so. . . . He's gonna text me, and he'll meet me out back and take me as far as Ukiah. I should be able to hitch from there . . . lots of trucks on the 101."

My heart twinges. "So . . . you'll work at this hostel and do all your network things, then go to Alaska . . . and then what?"

Sim leans away from me. "What do you mean, 'then what?'"

"Are you going to go to college, or do your equivalency exam, or anything like that?" *Are you ever coming back?*

Sim laughs. "Oh. Yeah. I took the equivalency exam last quarter, but my dad wouldn't let me leave school. Says a diploma looks better to colleges, so I stuck it out on the off chance I ever go. But, Lainey, this is *it*. This is what people *do*. They just . . . go out and live life, I guess."

Yeah. Life. That great big thing I know nothing about.

Even though we're close together, I sense a huge gulf between us in the silence that follows.

"I don't know, Lainey," Sim says finally. His voice is quiet in the darkness. "I don't know what happens next. But anything's got to be better than this."

Just about from the first day we moved to San Rosado, I've known Simeon Keller. These last two weeks, he's been everywhere. Even when I was irritated with him, feeling stupid and excluded from his life, he was in my thoughts. It's hard to imagine school without him. On Monday, I'll walk into Mr. Wilcox's physics classroom and know not to expect him ever again. For the first time since sixth grade . . . The thought hits me hard, and my eyes start to sting.

Come on, Laine. This is Simeon, I try to tell myself. He's annoying and self-centered and basically ignores me, but for a long time, even before I had a crush on him, he was my very best friend. My eyes overflow as I realize how much I'm going to miss him. On the other side of the bed, I know Sim's still awake. I can feel him leaving already. All of his big plans to take off are percolating in his brain, and even though he's right next to me, it's like he's already gone.

"Laine? Are you crying?"

I try to get out the word "no," but all that happens is that my breath catches in my throat. I quickly wipe my thumb beneath my eyes.

"Hey. *Hey.*" Sim pushes up on his elbow and taps on my shoulder. "Don't cry, Laine."

I take a deep breath and keep my back toward him. It hurts too much to talk. Why does he have to be so nice now? Why can't he be the jerk I've gotten used to?

Sim places a hesitant hand on my side and slides it under my arm. He pulls me back against him, brushing my hair away from his face with his other hand. His chin is on my shoulder.

"Did I do something?"

I shake my head, speechless.

"Is . . . did you have a bad dream?" Sim sounds honestly bewildered and out of his depth, which makes me laugh a little.

"I'm fine," I croak. I grab a tissue from my bedside table and blow my nose. I can think more clearly without hearing his voice vibrate through his chest. "I'm just . . . tired."

"Oh." Sim seems uneasy. "You sure? Laine, if you want, I can go now. I . . . I know your mom would freak, and if this is bugging you or . . ."

"No." I turn toward him, my eyes dripping again. "Don't go, Sim. Please." By the dim glow of the nightlight in my bathroom, I can see the uncertainty on his face. I try to cut back on the drama. "I mean, who knows when I'm going to see you again, right? So . . . I want you to stay. With me. Until you have to . . . to go."

Sim reaches out and brushes his fingers across the wetness on my cheeks. "Okay."

I close my eyes and bite the inside of my mouth, hard. Everything he does makes me feel like crying, and if I keep crying, I'm going to freak him out.

When I open my eyes, Sim has his head pillowed on his arms, watching me.

"What are you thinking about?" I ask. I wipe my nose one last time and slide back beneath the covers.

"Nothing." Sim's gaze is disconcerting.

"I got the money, if that's what you're worried about."

"It wasn't, but thanks." Sim leans forward suddenly and brushes my cheek with his lips. "I owe you one."

I put my hand on my cheek, covering the spot. "You always say that. But you're leaving, you know. I'm never going to collect."

Sim bites his bottom lip. "You will," he says quietly. "I'll make it up to you, Laine. I promise."

I smile. He always says that too, but for once it doesn't annoy me. Instead, it makes me sad again. I close my eyes against the stinging. "Good night, Sim."

"Night, Laine."

I roll over on my stomach and close my eyes. I feel Sim's fingers fumble for mine. His hands are still cold. I thread my fingers through his and hold on.

It doesn't seem like there's any way I'll ever go to sleep, but the next thing I hear is the bathroom door closing quietly, and the green numbers on the clock say it's six-fifteen. I stumble quietly out of bed, rubbing my eyes.

In the kitchen, I put the kettle on the stove, being careful to open the spigot so it won't whistle when it boils. This is it. In just a little while, Sim will be gone for good.

The kettle boils, and I make tea. I don't know what else to do. My hands feel empty, so I open the bread box and take out a bag of wheat rolls left over from the restaurant. I put four of them in the toaster oven on low. Then I get out a pot of mustard and look carefully at the eggs. I take four from the end of the crate and shake them one by one, carefully. Yep. They're boiled.

In *The Way to Cook,* Saint Julia guarantees the *perfect* hard-boiled egg with just a few simple steps that I have learned so well I can do them in my sleep. I started boiling eggs and leaving them in the fridge for a few days when MaDea told me that you couldn't make deviled eggs with really fresh eggs. It's true. They stick to the shell and look nasty when you try and peel them. It's ironic that week-old eggs work better. Since Mom knows where to shop, our eggs are *fresh,* fresh. The best thing I can do is to boil them and then let them age awhile in the safety of our refrigerator. It doesn't always work, but that's okay—the deviled eggs are tasty, even if they're not as pretty as MaDea's.

My chest doesn't feel so tight now that my hands are occupied with safe, familiar tasks. The eggs peel cleanly for once, and I take out a small bowl into which I lob all the yolks and a teaspoon of mustard. The whites I leave on the cutting board to chop later on.

I pull out green olives, sun-dried tomato tapenade, some scallions, and mayonnaise from the fridge. For now I skip the traditional celery and pickle route and go with some Hungarian paprika from the cabinet. There's a bit of fresh parsley left in the glass on the top shelf of the fridge, and I bring that along too.

I can smell the bread toasting. I quickly slice a scallion, then chop it finely with the parsley. I hope it isn't too strong. I take a couple tablespoons of mayo and two table-spoons of tapenade and mash all of that into the yolks. I add a dash of paprika and wonder if I should put in pick-les after all. I make a face. No. The whites chop quickly, and I dust the salad with a bit of white pepper and salt and then taste. It wakes up my sluggish taste buds.

It's almost seven. I've taken the rolls out of the toaster oven, sliced them open halfway, and stuffed the creamy egg salad inside them. I quickly wrap each of them in foil to keep them warm, then fill a zip-top bag with some of Mom's stash of pecan bark, a couple of gra-nola bars, and a few oranges. I can't think of anything else to pack that will keep well while Simeon is walking. I know he'll buy something when he needs to, but I want to give him as much as he can carry. No, food isn't love, and I know it. But it's the best I can do right now.

I glance at the clock, then up the stairs. I'm out of time.

Sim flinches when I come into the room. I've opened the door so quietly I've surprised him. He gives me a nervous smile and flicks his fingers through his damp hair. "Hey," he whispers.

My throat is tight. "Hey." I cough a little. "Did he text you yet?"

"Yep."

"Oh." I try to keep the smile on my face and hold out the bag. "Made you breakfast."

"Thanks." Sim takes the bag. "You didn't have to."

I shrug, cross my arms. "Oh." I move to the dresser and open my sock drawer. "Here."

Sim doesn't even look at the money, just shoves it in his pocket as if he's embarrassed. "Thanks. Listen, about your grandma's stuff." Sim stuffs the lunch bag into his coat pocket and turns toward me. "My folks will get it back to you guys; it's still in the boxes, even."

"That's no problem."

Sim glances toward the bathroom, then looks out the window.

"Is that him?"

"Not yet."

I breathe a sigh of relief.

Sim crosses the room to stand in front of me. "I'd better climb out anyway. If he doesn't see me, he might decide to just go on. Look. I'll give you a call once I'm on the road, drop you an e-mail or something. As soon as I'm settled, I'll let you know."

I nod jerkily and swallow hard. This shouldn't be as

big a deal as it feels. I'm almost eighteen, and I'm going to save up and travel after school is out. I'll find out where he is and come visit. Why does it feel like I will never see him again?

Sim steps forward awkwardly and puts his arms around me. "Well, here goes," he says with forced brightness. "Wish me luck, huh?"

I hold him tightly and breathe deep, relieved that I'm not going to cry. "Good luck."

Sim steps back. "Thanks, Laine," he says, his face serious. "I'm going to miss you."

Impulsively, I stand on tiptoe and kiss him. He's not expecting it, and I see his eyes widen a fraction of a second before I touch him, butterfly light, on his lips with my own.

He blinks and flinches like he's been burned.

I swallow and step back involuntarily. "S-sorry," I stammer. "I—"

Simeon bends forward and cups my face in one hand and puts his other hand on the back of my neck, under my hair. His hands are cold, but his lips are warm, and the feeling that I'm going to break down and cry gets derailed in the sensation of being cold and hot all over at once. Sim slides his hand down my back.

It's no more than a long moment, but both of us step backward a little stunned. For a few seconds, Simeon is still so close I can see his pupils, huge and dark.

"Sim. I . . ." I don't know what I was going to say.

"Laine." Sim shakes his head and trails a finger across my mouth. "I should—"

I find my voice. "Sim. You don't have to go. You could stay with us, with . . . with me. I know things with your parents aren't good, but . . . it's just . . ." My throat is closing again. I bite my tongue before the words *What am I going to do now?* get spoken. "I'll miss you," I whisper finally.

Sim turns toward the window. "Laine . . . I can't. I really *can't.*"

I'm struggling to swallow, and the tears I've been holding back are close. "Sim . . . stay. We could figure something out." I reach out and grab his hand.

"I can't stay here. I don't want to." The expression on my face—the pain—makes him look away. "I'm going," he says, and squeezes my hand. Then he lets go. He walks into the bathroom, pulls open the window, and climbs out into the dimness of the morning. The curtains flutter like waving hands behind him.

SAINT JULIA'S "PERFECTLY HARD-BOILED" EGG SALAD

4 HARD-BOILED EGGS **

2 TBSP. MAYONNAISE

5 OR 6 PIMENTO-STUFFED GREEN OLIVES, CHOPPED
   (OR 2 TBSP. OLIVE TAPENADE)

1 SMALL SHALLOT (OPTIONAL), FINELY CHOPPED

1 TSP. DIJON MUSTARD

1/8 TSP. PAPRIKA

1 TBSP. SWEET PICKLE RELISH (OR SUNDRIED TOMATO, OR TAPENADE)

1 TBSP. FRESH PARSLEY, FINELY CHOPPED * (OR CILANTRO)

TO TASTE: SALT AND FRESHLY GROUND BLACK PEPPER
   (ABOUT 1/8 TO 1/4 TSP OF EACH)

PEEL YOUR EGGS - IN THE SINK, TO KEEP THE SHELLS CLOSE TO
THE DISPOSAL. CAREFULLY TAKE OUT YOUR YOLKS, AND SET THE
WHITES ASIDE. ADD TO YOUR YOLKS THE MAYONNAISE, YOUR
                    SHALLOTS
CHOPPED OLIVES, THE MUSTARD, PAPRIKA, AND PICKLE. THEN
CHOP YOUR WHITES, AND ADD TO MIXTURE. ADD PARSLEY,
                    FRESH
SALT, AND A LITTLE GROUND BLACK PEPPER TO TASTE.
* YOU CAN USE CILANTRO AND SUNDRIED TOMATOES AS A
VARIATION. SOME PEOPLE LIKE THEIR BREAD COLD FOR COOL
EGG SALAD. — FOR A FRESH EGG SALAD, YOU MIGHT USE
WARM ROLLS. YUM.

** SAINT JULIA'S NOTES ON BOILING EGGS ARE EASY. ALL YOU HAVE TO DO IS MAKE SURE YOUR EGGS ARE COVERED AT LEAST AN INCH DEEP IN COLD WATER IN THE POT, SO MAKE YOUR POT DEEP, NOT FLAT AND WIDE. BOIL FOR EXACTLY 17 MINUTES. TRANSFER THE BOILED EGGS TO ICE WATER IMMEDIATELY TO CHILL FOR 2 MINUTES. TAKE THEM BACK INTO THE BOILING WATER FOR 10 SECONDS; THIS WILL MAKE SURE YOUR YOLKS AREN'T GREEN AND THAT THE EGGS WON'T STICK TO THE SHELLS. NOW MOVE THEM BACK INTO THE COLD, AND LET THEM SIT - IF YOU CAN - FOR 15 MINUTES. IF YOU CAN'T, IT DOESN'T MATTER, BUT COLD EGGS PEEL BETTER.

11

"Where's my boning knife?"

Pia is shouting, and tension is high in the kitchen at La Salle. There's a food critic in the restaurant from *Taste the North Bay,* and all the chefs are in a huge panic. I'm actually being treated like a real chef's assistant, which means Stefan just screamed at me for overbeating a bowl of egg whites he was going to use for a sour cherry soufflé. I didn't even know you could overbeat egg whites, but he's just ranted and raved and banged his big fist on the counter about did I just think I was making meringue and now he's going to make me do it all over again—by *hand*. It's all I can do not to burst out crying.

I am so tired of crying.

I feel fragile, like broken glass that's been badly mended with glue that isn't yet dry. I want to sit very, very still for a while until the feeling that I might shatter goes away. The rumor mill at school has been very busy with news of who's in trouble, who's sent to military school, and that type of thing. People are talking about Sim. No one has come up to me and asked, but I've gotten some looks lately like people are wondering if I know something. Even if I did, I wouldn't tell them.

It's been three days.

Eventually, I had to wash my face. I felt like some middle school kid, thinking she'd never wash her hand again because some boy she likes touched it. I am not that lame. Quite. I won't wash my sweatshirt yet; I know that much. It still smells like him.

"Seifert! I need those whites yesterday!" Stefan is bellowing, and I pull myself back into the moment. There's barely room in my little corner of the world to stand, but I hunker into my work space and start over. First, I clean the bowl, since egg whites won't whip in a dirty bowl. With a mixture of a quarter cup of vinegar and a tablespoon of salt, I rinse it and dry it thoroughly with paper towels before cracking four eggs in a separate bowl and making sure there are no yolks in my white. The eggs are room temperature, and I use the balloon whisk Stefan gave me to beat them, incorporating air into the liquid. It takes me a little while to get it right. At first I'm moving my wrist too much. After a little while, I find a rhythm that is comfortable for me.

The bowl is tipped to the side, and I move the whisk in tight circles.

"Where are the whites, Elaine!"

"I'm coming!" I want to throw something.

After the egg whites begin to foam, I carefully add a half teaspoon of cream of tartar to help stabilize things. I want to dump it in, but I'm scared now. I don't want to have to do this again. I keep moving the whisk, counting under my breath. I'm trying to make a hundred beats per minute, but I can't go that fast.

It seems like hours later when the whites stiffen into soft peaks. My arm is killing me, and I hate Stefan. I hate cherries. I hate soufflé. I hate everyone. I keep whipping. Should I stop? It doesn't look over-whipped to me, but what do I know? What do I know about anything?

Stefan stalks to my workstation and holds out his hand.

"What?" I stop moving and glare. I know my voice is surly and wobbly.

Stefan raises his eyebrows, then takes my whisk and dips it.

"Soft peaks," he says gruffly. "That's what you need for soufflé. Next time do it like this the first time." Stefan takes the bowl and thumps me on the shoulder. "Clean your workstation."

I close my eyes and take a deep breath. I want to be a chef. I will not break down and bawl because Stefan didn't tell me how great I am. Saint Julia survived the Cordon Bleu. I open my eyes and grimly start cleaning up.

I can't believe how much I don't want to be here. This kitchen used to be everything to me, and now all I want to do is curl up in my bed and hide.

Monday night Mom came home, worry written all over her face. She'd had another phone call from Mrs. Keller, she said. The scene still plays in my head:

"Lainey . . . Honey, they still haven't heard from Simeon. . . ."

I looked at my hands. I couldn't look at her face.

"I told Mrs. Keller I'd call if he came by our place, but, Lainey, she sounds so awful. . . . Do you have *any* idea where he is?"

Mom asked the question in a way that enabled me to avoid a direct lie. "No idea, Mom. None."

I rinse out the copper bowl again, drying it carefully. "Ana Haines called and canceled her standing Monday night reservation—apparently Christopher got up to something. . . . And now apparently there's some kind of missing-persons report going out on Simeon. The Kellers haven't seen him since last Friday." I remember how she'd frowned down at me. "It just doesn't seem like Simeon to not be around somewhere. . . . You haven't heard anything?"

I'd dodged the question. "Nobody's seen him?"

"Well, Mrs. Keller said that she'd just come home

157

from being away and that Simeon wasn't in the house, and later on, she found that his things were gone. . . . Laine, I'm worried."

I blurted, "I am too. I haven't heard anything from him since Friday when—" I closed my mouth.

My mother was staring at me. "Wait. You just said you had no idea . . ."

I shook my head. "I don't. I just—"

Mom was angry. "Elaine, if you know *anything*, you should have said. Their child is missing. And no matter what you or I might think of things in that household, it's just not right not to let them know that we've at least seen him alive and in one piece more recently than they have."

I tried to explain. I told my mom about the Kellers, and how cranky Mrs. Keller was, and how Simeon didn't get along with them, but in the end nothing I said stopped Mom from picking up the phone and dialing after giving me this huge lecture about social responsibility. I was furious with myself for being so stupid.

"Mrs. Keller? Vivianne Seifert again. I just wanted to let you know that Elaine saw Simeon this past Friday."

"Well, of course you can speak to her. Elaine?" My mother handed me the phone and sat down expectantly.

I'd felt like I had a mouthful of sawdust. What was I supposed to say?

Unexpectedly, it was *Mr.* Keller who interrogated me like I was on trial. Why hadn't I told them anything before? Where was Simeon now? What time had I seen him? Had I been at the party with the other kids?

Party? I blessed Sim again for not inviting me. "No, sir. I wasn't at the party," I told Mr. Keller, and Mom's eyebrows furrowed. I could see the wheels turning in her head, and the look she gave me wasn't promising. Mr. Keller asked to speak to Mom again. I handed her the phone and made a move to get up. Mom grabbed my arm and shook her head.

"Yes, Vivianne Seifert here. Yes, Mr. Keller.

"I *beg your pardon*? Mr. Keller, are you threatening my daughter?

"I see. Mr. Keller, you are obviously upset, and I will take your comments with that consideration in mind. Good night." Mom hung up abruptly and then sat for a moment, glaring at the floor. I expected to see the hardwood go up in smoke. She was still holding on to my arm and just sitting.

"Mom?"

Mom hadn't looked up. "Elaine, you need to explain something to me. That man just insinuated that you are 'obstructing justice' and 'aiding and abetting a criminal' and said he'd sue us if he finds out that we are 'hiding' his son! Will you please tell me what's going on?"

A criminal. They're calling Sim a criminal.

My mother is freaking out about this whole thing. She asked me a bunch of questions about that party at Sim's. I guess the Kellers didn't tell her the details either. Now that she knows that someone brought some marijuana and a keg, she's acting like I'm the one who's on drugs. And when she heard that people got arrested, she hit the roof.

"Drugs and alcohol and *arrests!*" she said, all upset. "Isabelle Elaine, you *know better* than this! I thought I could *trust you!*"

"Mom, it wasn't me! It was probably all Carrigan's friends; I've told you about him." I remembered Sim's huge pupils and looked away.

"I have been afraid for some time that Simeon Keller is a negative influence on you. I trusted both of your judgment, and I see I was wrong. When he comes home, Elaine, I'm not sure what kind of relationship I'm prepared for you to have."

"*Mom!*" I said. "Are you *listening* to yourself? You're not making sense."

"Making sense? Does it make sense that drugs and police and God-knows-what-all-else has been going on without my knowledge?"

That did it. I started crying and screaming that she couldn't take away my friends and that she sounded like a psycho and that I didn't deserve this. I surprised her when I started crying. I surprised myself. I was sobbing so hard she could hardly understand the words.

We finally both got a little more calmed down, but only after she made me go through it all over again.

"Okay. Now, tell me again. There was a party; there were drugs and alcohol; there were cops. Simeon didn't test positive for anything."

"No."

"And you have not been drinking or doing drugs."

"Mother."

"Humor me, Isabelle Elaine. I need to hear it."

"No and *no* and NO. I *do* not and *have* not and *will* not. This was at Simeon's party, remember? I didn't even go."

My mother glared at me, and I responded to her unspoken reminder to modify my tone. "I'm sorry. But, Mom, I'm the same person I always am. I haven't done drugs; I've never seen Sim doing drugs; this was all just something that happened at a party that got out of hand. I promise." My promises were getting to be as frequent and meaningless as Sim's.

It was late, and Mom was tired. I felt guilty when I realized just how exhausted she must be. She'd been schmoozing and smiling all evening at the restaurant, and this wasn't something good to come home to, I knew. I tried to make it up to her, but it was still sitting between us three days later.

"Take a break, Lainey." Stefan calls me back to the present. "Twenty minutes, okay?"

In my mother's office, I sit down at her desk. I check e-mail automatically, but there isn't any message from Simeon, and I pull up a sudoku game and begin fiddling with the numbers.

I've called Sim's cell every day since he left. I just leave him a short message that I hope he's okay, but I don't expect him to call. I'm still embarrassed that I begged him so hard to stay. He's probably thinking leaving was a good thing.

"Laine?" Mom is in the doorway.

"Hey. Stefan said I could take a break." I stand up. "Need the computer?"

"No." Mom drops into the chair across the desk. "Laine." She sighs. "Have you heard from Simeon?"

It feels like Pia's boning knife is stuck in my throat. "No."

"Lord." Mom looks over at me and sighs, rubbing a weary hand over her forehead. "I was hoping he'd called someone."

"Not me," I say quietly. I can't have this conversation anymore. I head toward the door.

"Oh, Laine," Mom says sympathetically. "I'm sorry." She stands and touches my back, slides an arm around my shoulders. "I'm sorry, sweetheart. I forget how hard this must be on you too."

"Thank you." My voice sounds small. I lean into her half hug. She's still upset and really shaken by the idea of drugs and Sim, but now she's more worried about me than angry with me. I think, *If you knew the whole story, would you still be so sympathetic?*

I refuse to let myself dwell on the truth: I'm not as good a daughter as she thinks.

I could come clean. If this were a movie, the writers could put in a part where I could tell the truth about where Sim's going, and Mom would be relieved that I had used my savings to help him. Sure, she'd rant awhile about people who run away and how unsafe the world is for people our age, but after she got it out of her system, she'd be supportive. She's on my side now, mine and Sim's. I could tell her where he is, where he's headed, at least, and someone else could share the responsibility of knowing he's out there in the world alone. Someone stronger than I am would care if he's okay. There are only a few words between Sim and safety.

I open my mouth.

"You know, I was just going to make some hot chocolate. You want some?"

A little sugar to make the bitterness ease. It's foolproof.

COCOA AZTECA

1/4 C. GRANULATED SUGAR OR <u>4 TBSP.</u> SUGAR SUBSTITUTE

DASH OF SALT

1/4 C. DUTCH PROCESS COCOA POWDER, UNSWEETENED

(WOULD GROUND COCOA NIBS OR MICRO-PLANED BAKING ~~MICROPLANED BAKING~~ CHOCOLATE WORK?)

1/4 TSP. FRESH GROUND CINNAMON (REAL VIETNAMESE CASSIA IS BEST)

1/4 TSP. CAYENNE PEPPER (EXPERIMENT WITH MORE IF YOU'RE

FEELING ADVENTUROUS!)

3 C. MILK (YOU CAN USE SKIM MILK IF YOU WANT)

1/2 TSP. VANILLA EXTRACT (TRY ALMOND EXTRACT — Y<u>UM</u>!)

COMBINE SUGAR, SALT, COCOA, AND SPICES IN SMALL, HEAVY-DUTY
SAUCEPAN; GRADUALLY STIR IN MILK. WARM OVER MEDIUM HEAT,
STIRRING CONSTANTLY, UNTIL HOT (DO NOT BOIL). REMOVE FROM
HEAT; STIR IN VANILLA OR ALMOND EXTRACT.

* * IF YOU USE ~~2%~~ WHOLE OR 2% MILK, BEATING IT WITH
A WIRE WHISK WILL MAKE IT FROTHY! * *

* * USE 1 TBSP. SUGAR OR SUBSTITUTE, 2 TSP. COCOA POWDER, AND 1 C. MILK
FOR INDIVIDUAL SERVINGS. SEASON WITH VANILLA, CAYENNE,
AND SALT TO TASTE.

* * TO MAKE POWDERED MIX FOR CAMPING, USE 1 C. DRY
MILK MIX, ADDING 4 C. HOT BOILING WATER.

12

The doorbell rings sometime after noon on Sunday, and I hear a familiar voice. MaDea.

Conflicting feelings of happiness and wariness propel me into a quick shower. By the time I get downstairs, my grandmother and Mom are deep into gospel CDs and eating lunch, sitting comfortably tucked up by the fireplace. They stop talking when I come in, and the way my mother looks at me tells me that my wish for her to just "get it over with" has been answered. My heart sinks.

"Hey, Mom. Hey, Dee," I greet them, trying for an enthusiasm I don't feel. I sit on the back of the couch and lean down to hug my grandmother, who smells like citrus peels and rose petals.

"Well, good afternoon." My grandmother smiles, resplendent in her pearl gray velour tracksuit, a paisley silk scarf knotted around her throat. I smile at that paisley scarf. My beautiful, stylish grandmother always makes me smile, even when she makes Mom sigh and roll her eyes.

"Elaine, did you get any breakfast?" my mother asks neutrally, eyes on my eyes. She's wearing her usual weekend uniform of clogs and faded flannel, much like I am. Dea makes us both look orphaned and under-dressed.

"I had something." I shrug and lean down to look into Dea's plate. I don't like the way Mom is staring at me, like she's trying to read headlines in my face.

"Something decent, I hope? A girl can worry herself to skin and bone about a boy, you know." Dea's smooth brow has a little pucker in it, and I can see my face reflected in the panes of her glasses.

I tense, and I can sense Mom picking up on my tension like a leopard scenting prey. Now I know how much Mom has told Dea and that this isn't going to be pretty. Simeon's troubles are about to become a family matter.

"I'm not worried; I just wasn't all that hungry," I blurt, trying to forestall my mother launching into the Conversation. "I'm ready to eat, though." I push off from the couch and take a step toward the kitchen. "What's there to eat?"

"Your grandmother brought you some cottage cheese

loaf, and I brought home that mushroom soup of Pia's that you like, if you want that." Even when she's upset with me, my mother is never one to miss an opportunity to push food into my face. "And come on over here and sit with us when you've filled your plate," she goes on. "We need to talk about this. You've been holed up in your room for long enough."

"Yes, ma'am." That isn't an invitation, so I decide to take as long as I can. I make a salad.

Cabbage heads are the best thing on earth to whack against the counter really hard when you're trying to drown out the sound of your mother talking about you to your grandmother. I chop about a cup of red cabbage and pulverize the remaining wedge of regular green that was in the crisper drawer until I get out some of my aggression.

"Elaine? What is that racket?"

"I'm making cabbage slaw. Um, I'm about done." Unfortunately, it really is so easy a dish that I can't linger over it for long. The cottage cheese casserole smells so good I have to sneak a piece before I put it on my plate. Yum. Flavored with caramelized onions and mushrooms and bulked out with panko bread crumbs, it's one of Dea's best experimental-vegetarian-granddaughter recipes yet. I have got to learn how to make this.

I dish up, sprinkle the crunchies on my salad, then

come around the bar counter into the living room and pull out a stool. Mom said to come back and sit, but I'm not going to cuddle down on the couch between her and Dea for the Inquisition. *No, thank you.*

We all nibble from our plates for a while, and Dea says some innocuous things about the cold snap we're having and the ladies in her church. Mom answers something else, mumble, mumble, and we let the voices of the choir glide between us. Finally, Dea sets her plate on the edge of the table.

"Can I get you something else, MaDea?" If only we could all just keep eating.

"Not right now, baby. If you like that cottage cheese loaf, I wrote the recipe for you."

"Thank you, Dee. Mine won't taste this good, though."

"Hmph." My grandmother smiles smugly. She really is an excellent cook, and she doesn't mind being reminded. She could have had a cooking show, but there wasn't even cable back in her day, not to mention a place for an African American woman chef on TV.

"You ever cook for that boy?"

I'm yanked back from my thoughts. "Simeon?"

"Elaine, who else?" my mother snaps, suddenly losing her air of civility. "I know I did not raise a *stupid* child, so stop acting like one and tell me *exactly* what went on here last week."

Has she found out something? I open my mouth, but I'm saved by Dea's placid tones.

"Now, Vivianne, you're making a mountain out of what might be a little bitty molehill. Give the child a moment to answer before you go jumping all down her throat."

I swallow. "Mom, I told you."

"Well, Elaine, tell me again."

A little spurt of anger flickers along my cheeks, making my face go hot. I set down my fork.

I'm starting to feel like she's interrogating me, asking me to tell her over and over again to see if I change my story. It takes all I have to keep my temper.

"I *told you* I was making myself some food and then Sim came in with his key, and then I told you I gave him dinner, and *he left.* And that was over a week ago, and I don't know where he is right now, I don't know who he's with, I don't know where he slept last night, and I don't know if he's coming back." I'm bordering on disrespectful.

Mom is leaning forward on the couch. "And what did you make him for dinner Friday night?"

The question seems odd. "I told you, Mom, when you called. I made soup and latkes."

"And rolls?" Mom asks.

"Rolls? N—" And then I see the trap I've walked into. "I made him some sandwiches. For later."

"From rolls I brought home after midnight on Friday," my mother says flatly.

I'm dead.

"Did you count all the eggs in the fridge too?" I push my plate back with shaking hands. "It's not a crime to eat something, Mom."

"So, you knew he was running away, and you packed him a lunch, did you? In the morning? Where did he stay the night?"

"I didn't say he was running away! He didn't say he was running away either. He's just . . . gone. I don't know when he's coming back. He didn't say." I close my mouth, afraid now. It is too easy to give things away.

"Elaine," my grandmother interjects. "Do you know why your mother is so concerned? Your mother is concerned because there's been a car . . . sitting outside of this house, since she went out to get the paper this morning. There's a man. . . ."

I jerk off the stool and move toward the front window. "What? A man? Is it Mr. Keller? Where?"

My mother pulls me back from the drapes. "Lainey, don't point. . . . I already called the police. He's an investigator; the Kellers hired him privately. He's just watching . . . to make sure Simeon isn't here."

"Seriously?" I pull away from my mother so she can't see how badly I'm shaking. "That's crazy. Mom, this is ridiculous!"

"No, it is not ridiculous. Lainey, the investigator has pulled phone records for Simeon and knows that you've made a lot of calls to his cell phone. They know that boy came over here, and they know the two of you have been as thick as thieves since you were little kids."

Stop calling him "that boy." His name is Simeon. His name is Simeon. You can't have forgotten already.

"His parents are going to be watching you, and I wouldn't be surprised if they watched the school, our house, his apartment, the coffee shop where he worked, the restaurant. . . ."

It's suddenly hard to breathe, and my throat feels like someone has rubbed it with sandpaper. "But, Mom, *I told you.* He isn't here and I don't know where he is. Do they think something happened to him?" My stomach crawls.

My mother rubs a hand over her face and softens her tone as she tries to herd me back toward the couch. "Elaine, if they hired an investigator, they're not playing around. The police haven't been by to ask us any questions, so we can probably assume that there are no criminal charges, but this investigator represents some serious intentions—and some serious cash. The Kellers want to find their son. And that's why I want you to think again, dear heart, think it through all the way and make sure that you have nothing to do with this, Lainey. We haven't got the kind of money it would take to fight off a lawsuit from the likes of them."

"Money?" Is that what this is about? Doesn't she hear what she's saying? The Kellers want their son back, but when does he stop being theirs to have?

"It's not just the money," Mom says. She stops walking and looks into my face. "It's just the principle of the thing, Lainey. I don't like you getting so involved in a family that's so . . . unstable."

Unstable describes exactly how I feel right now. I want to slide down the wall. Instead, I stumble across the tiles to the stairs and sit there, trying to get some distance.

Everybody's asking me to say something to get Simeon "back where he belongs." More than anything in my life right now, I want him back, but even if he were here, things wouldn't be the same. Everything had so much potential just a week ago. But now . . .

I can't stay here. I don't want to.

"Elaine, don't cry. I'm not trying to be unkind—I know Simeon's your friend. I'm not accusing you of hiding him. I just thought if you would tell me again, from the top, what happened, maybe I could get some idea of where he went or what he plans, and maybe we could—"

"*Mom*, I *don't* know!" I beat my fist on my knees in frustration, feeling the truth piling up behind my clenched teeth. "He came over, I gave him some food, and . . . and we talked, and he told me he just wanted to have a normal life, and I just can't—" I wave my hands

172

in the air, fighting for words. "How am I supposed to say that to his parents?"

Mom squats down in front of me, intent. I feel the power of her gaze and shrink back. She's trying to psych me out, I can tell. My flannel shirt seems too warm.

"Tell them what? What can't you tell them, Elaine?"

I look at my mother coldly. "Aren't you listening?"

"Did you give him any money?" My grandmother's voice slides in between us, and I flinch. My mother sinks her face into her hands. "Oh, Lainey, no . . ."

"Mom, *please,* it wasn't much. He didn't have any money. I just wanted to be sure he slept someplace warm, okay? He was going to leave no matter what. He wouldn't go home. I couldn't make him go home."

A tear leaks from my right eye into my mouth, and I swallow it like a little kid. Simeon didn't even think of this part, but the disappointment and unhappiness in my mother's face catches me like an unexpected punch to the gut.

"So, you gave him money, and you made him food." Dea's voice is soft. "Is that all?"

"That's all. MaDea, you don't know him, but he wasn't bad, he just wanted to get away. He told me right before he left that he was just going—" My thoughts flounder. "Just going to hitchhike," I finish abruptly. "I don't even know who picked him up. I didn't see the car."

My mother glances at her mother, her back stiff. "And that's all?"

"That's *all*, Mom."

"Well, I know you did what you thought best." Dea stands up from the couch and crosses the room toward me. "There's not too much you can tell a boy when they're that age, though, is there?" Dea's knees creak as she sits down on the stair next to me.

"This boy . . ." Mom sighs, her eyes closed, as she leans against the wall.

"What?" I'm quivery and nervous, tired of feeling on edge.

My mother opens her eyes. "I've always thought it was nice that you were his friend, but I've also wished you spent your time with some other kids. Whatever happened between you and Lorraine? Or why don't you get on with Ana's boy anymore?"

I glance up angrily. "Lorraine? Mom, you know *why* she was friends with me? Because she wanted to hook up with SIMEON, okay? And Christopher—look, I've got other friends, Mom, okay? I don't need you to help me with this."

My mother takes a deep breath and rubs her hands as if she's dusting them clean. "Elaine . . . I've been doing some thinking. I really think it would be a positive thing if you started looking ahead to your life and working to- ward your goals and dreams. You filled out only a couple of applications for college . . . why don't we work on some school tours, see what else is out there? Or maybe you want to travel. There's a lot out there in the world for a girl your age instead of thinking about going straight through from school to the restaurant business."

What does Mom mean, it might be "a positive thing" if I was working toward the goals of my life? I've been thinking about having my cooking show forever. "What?"

"I've been thinking that maybe you'd enjoy going down south this summer, maybe stay with your great-aunt May and take some classes at a junior college or something."

"What? No offense, Dea, to your sister, but I'm not going. Mom, there's no way."

My mother's chin goes up, and her eyebrows clamp down. "Laine, you are not telling me where you will and will not go. Obviously I haven't been watching you well enough here. You need more supervision, and La Salle isn't the place—"

I'm on my feet, hands clenched. "Mother, I am almost eighteen. I know what I'm doing this summer, and it's not going somewhere so I can be babysat by some people I don't even know."

"Elaine. Vivianne. Both of you sit down. You look like bantam roosters." MaDea is sitting on the stairs shaking her head.

I glare at my grandmother. "MaDea, I'm sorry, but I think Mom just asked you to come down today so you could help her make me do what she wants. It's not going to work."

"Isabelle Elaine, I don't know *whose* house you think you're living in," my mother begins.

"So now you want me to move out?" My voice is too high.

Dea pats my leg and clambers to her feet. "Now, you-all pipe down. Laine, you have no idea how much you sound like your *mother* when she was your age. Come on back to the table now, both of you. I brought cobbler and peach ice cream . . . oh, and some of that healthful soy ice cream for you, Miss Lainey."

"Wait a minute," Mom says to me quietly. She leans forward and brings her eyes level with mine. "I know it doesn't seem fair, Elaine, and I apologize, but you are my only child, and you will succeed in this world even if I have to drag you kicking and screaming."

I shrug, arms crossed.

"I've been concerned about you and Simeon, and I'd made up my mind to get to know him better if he was going to be spending time here . . . without his shirt on." Now Mom smiles humorlessly.

My throat constricts. That seems light-years ago.

"No matter how all of this comes out," my mother

continues, and I can feel my eyes stinging and a lone drop making its way out of my nose, "I think you should spend some time working on your goals. As a matter of fact, I'm going to insist you spend that time. Elaine, you've been chasing after this boy for how long? You've spent too long waiting on what he's going to do and where he's going to be. A great girl like you—there will be all kinds of people who are going to think you're the best thing that's ever happened to them. I'd like you to start thinking about where you'd like to do a summer internship. If you can get some distance from . . . everything, I'd like to see you start striking out on your own."

"How about Alaska?" The angry tone of my voice makes my mother step back. "Maybe that's the kind of distance I need."

Mom sighs. "Elaine . . ." She shakes her head. "We don't need the dramatics."

"I'm sure there's a restaurant there that needs an intern. And I'll be happy to go."

My mother's shoulders slump. "Lainey, you're taking this the wrong way."

"I'll be interning this summer somewhere away from home. Fine. I'll start looking."

"One day you'll thank me." My mother's voice is light, but I can see that she feels it's time to put in her last word and end this conversation. "I know you don't see what I mean about Simeon," she adds, "but take my word for it, this once. It will do you good to get away for a while. This hasn't been good for you." She sighs and places her hand on my tightly clenched fists. "Go wash your face, Lainey bug," she says as she gets up. "And come eat some of that nasty soy ice cream your grandmother keeps bringing you."

Deep breath. Mom is changing the menu, moving us all along to a new dish. She thinks she's managed me, managed this whole scene. This time, I'm going to let her think what she wants.

I go upstairs into the bathroom to wash my face like my mother says. Like a good girl.

Like the girl I'm not.

I run the sink tap and sit on the edge of the tub, burying my face in a towel.

"Is that peach homemade?" I hear Mom calling to Dea.

Downstairs, my mother and grandmother are serving up dessert. Upstairs, I'm crying so hard I want to vomit.

Everywhere I look, I'm being forced into lying. Simeon's making me lie to Mom. Mom's making me lie about Simeon. I have to go intern somewhere, and I will, and I may go there and stay a whole year, but right now I'm not even sure I want to be a chef anymore. I'm not sure of anything.

How did it end up like this? Sim went from being

my best friend to being the guy who only talked to me when he needed something. Why did I think this time he would be any different? Just because I wanted him to be?

I'm going to have to get a job. I'm never going to be able to take my trip to Saint Julia's, especially now that I'm five hundred dollars in the hole. I have to do something or Mom's going to manage everything, just like I'm still some little kid who doesn't have a clue.

What makes it worse is that she's right. I have been waiting for Simeon. I'm lying to my mother, I have investigators watching my house, and where is he?

Saint Julia always said that in cooking, there are very few mistakes that can't be corrected. You can add a pinch of salt and some chopped herbs to the butter if you forgot to put salt in your bread. If your soufflé falls, you can serve it with a sauce over it, and it'll look just fine. Gummy mashed potatoes can be resurrected as potato pancakes. But once you add too much pepper to something—it's over. You can't make something less spicy than it is.

I stand and rinse out my mouth. My stomach feels like a fist, knotted and quivering with tension.

Sim's history. And now I have to figure out what to do next.

AWESOME CABBAGE SLAW
—PIA'S RECIPE!

2 C. CABBAGE (USE BOTH RED AND GREEN FOR EXTRA COLOR...)
1 GREEN ONION (CHIFFONADED - CHIVES SNIPPED INTO BITS WORKS TOO.)
2 TBSP. (OR MORE!) GINGER - HABANERO SALAD DRESSING
1 TSP. (OR MORE) MAE PLOY SWEET PEPPER SAUCE
     (ASK PIA WHICH KIND - TABASCO WORKS ?.)
1/4 C. FRIED CHOW MEIN NOODLES
1/4 C. HONEY - ROASTED SOY NUTS
SCATTERED HANDFUL OF RAISINS OR DRIED CRANBERRIES
OR DRIED PINEAPPLE

USING A BOX GRATER OR A MANDOLINE GRATER, SHRED CABBAGE
FINELY. ADD TO BOWL CONTAINING FINELY SLICED ONIONS. DRESS
CABBAGE AND ONION WITH BE GINGER - HABANERO DRESSING;
ADD MAE PLOY SAUCE TO TASTE. GARNISH WITH CRUNCHY NOODLES
AND SOY NUTS, ADD OPTIONAL DRIED FRUIT.

＊＊ WATCH OUT FOR THE PEPPER SAUCE ! THIS CAN GET TOO SPICY
     FAST. ADD ANOTHER CUP OF CHOPPED CABBAGE IF THAT HAPPENS.
     OR 1 C. FRESH MEDIUM TOFU CHUNKS, LIGHTLY STIR-FRIED.
     OR MUSHROOMS. AND MORE CABBAGE.

13

"Lainey? Is that you?"

Who else? I throttle back the urge to snarl as I close the hallway door behind me. My mother has a heavy grasp on the obvious.

The mail is full of junk circulars and advertising, a King Arthur Flour catalog, and nothing from the *Just Tomatoes* recipe contest I entered two weeks ago. I throw everything on the kitchen counter and stomp up the stairs.

"Come here," Mom calls from her room. She sounds excited. "I've got something neat to show you."

I mutter expletives. It's been a horrible day already, and Mom's voice is so light and cheerful I know this "something neat" is going to be one of her Good Mother ideas. In the land of Mother-Daughter Quality Time, so far we've gone to Dea's church and fed the homeless, toured vineyards and art galleries in the Napa Valley, and even gone to Bingo Night at Dea's senior club. Mom tried to get me to go to a Women's Health fund-raiser at St. Joseph's with her and Mrs. Haines, but she let me get out of that when I said I had too much homework. I can't go anywhere anymore without her poking her nose in, smiling at everyone. When I'm at the restaurant, I see her watching me. She's even come to my gym, just popped in one day while I ran faster and faster on the treadmill, trying to get away.

I grind my teeth at her cheery little voice and clomp up the stairs to her doorway.

"Look!" My mother excitedly points to her computer screen. "It's the Elderwood Estates Cooking School. They have an opening during your spring break for a Wednesday-to-Friday course."

"Uh-huh." Sighing inaudibly, I glance at the computer and make my way down the hallway to my room.

"They've got vineyards and orchards and their own herb garden!" Mom continues. I can *hear* the exclamation points. I keep walking.

"Does that sound like someplace where you might like to intern?" Mom calls after me, oblivious to my disinterest.

I turn back to her room. "Maybe. I don't know. Why?"

Mom is typing something. "Well, I told you that you ought to be looking for places where you can get in and get a different kind of experience than you would at school," she says. "A cooking school like Elderwood is just one of many options for your summer."

My stomach curdles. "I said I'd find something for myself for summer."

Mom swivels around in her chair and sighs. "Well, get to it, Elaine. I need to know you have a plan."

"Why?" I look at her, bewildered.

Mom shakes her head. "It looks like this is going to be a busy summer. Pia's afraid we're going to get audited this year, and they've just announced that the *Michelin Guide* is coming back to the Bay Area—really, when Pia and I got into this, we made a decision to be in a partnership with this restaurant . . . and I'm not holding up my end. And since we debuted the new menu, we're getting reviewed again, and there's always so much to do this time of year . . . I just need to make sure everything's covered." Mom sighs a little and turns back toward her computer, looking pensive.

I turn down the hall and go to my room, opening the door, taking off my jacket. In a moment, Mom follows and props herself in the doorway.

"So, we need to explore internship opportunities for you," she continues as I plop down on the bed and stretch out.

"Whatever." I yawn. I'm tired, but I have miles to go

before I sleep. The midsemester schoolwork crunch has been kicking my butt lately, and I've got to catch up on my studying. Somehow with one thing and another, school's been the last thing on my mind.

"Laine." My mother sounds suddenly suspicious. "You don't have plans for spring break that I don't know about, do you?"

I open my eyes a crack. Is she joking? Isn't this the woman who's always complaining I have no social life and should cultivate more friends like the ever-wonderful Lorraine?

I stretch my arms over my head and sigh. "Of course, Mom, I'm going to Botswana on a safari. What makes you think I have a life all of a sudden?"

Instead of showing irritation at my snarky response, Mom's face clears of a tension I didn't know was there. She nods. "Well, that's good. . . . That's what I told Mrs. Keller. Their investigator is of the opinion that Simeon will be contacting friends over this break. I expect that little gray car will be parked out front again all week." She flashes me a humorless smile.

"Oh, great." I toe off my shoes and flop over onto my stomach. "Like our own Neighborhood Watch."

My mother sighs. "Well, Laine, that's how it goes. I'm not sure what good it will do them, but eventually, they're going to find out what they need to know." She pauses a moment. "I hope you've told Mr. Keller everything."

I feel a flash of annoyance. "Mom. You've been in my face practically every second for the last three weeks. You could tell Mr. Keller yourself: there's no one hiding under my bed. I already told you everything I knew."

My mother is silent for a moment too long. I look up at her and catch a weird expression on her face, part anger, part something else.

"What?"

Mom just shakes her head. "We're going back to the restaurant. Grab your books."

I sigh. "Mom . . ."

"No negotiations, Isabelle Elaine." Mom's voice is stiff. "This is the agreement."

In return for her not pressuring me about spending time with MaDea's sister in Baton Rouge, I agreed to find a summer internship and be "supervised" when I was outside of school. That means going to the restaurant with her, doing prep work, and doing homework in her office. It's not as bad as it sounds. When I get sick of it, I can stretch out on her love seat and plug in my music, but today I'm so tired not even that has any appeal.

"Fine." I sit up and slide my feet into my shoes. "This is the agreement, but it doesn't last forever, okay? It's not fair that I'm being punished when I haven't done anything wrong."

Mom gets a strange look on her face again and turns to go. "Just get a move on, Elaine."

*　　*　　*

Ms. Dunston is still sipping her coffee, and "Deep River," the spiritual we've been working on, is echoing in my brain. I'm humming along to myself, digging in my book bag for a highlighter, so Christopher Haines standing next to me barely registers.

"Hey, Elaine."

"You want something, Chris?"

Christopher jams his hands in his pockets and leans against the wall. "You're never going to call me Topher, are you?" He sighs, looking aggrieved.

I stifle the urge to laugh. Even with the baby dread-locks in his curly dark hair, the faded jeans, and the striped vintage shirt, Trendy Topher still looks like the clumsy little junior high kid I remember as Chris. Even though he was at Sim's party and supposedly got busted like everyone else, he's still geeky Chris to me.

"All right, Topher. What d'ya want?" I pull out the novel we're reading for English and hope I have a free moment to finish the assigned chapter. After getting yelled at some more by Stefan last night, I didn't feel like doing anything but flopping down and watching TV. The trend on cooking shows now is to convey the "reality" of a "real" kitchen. There's a lot more drama on TV: people get yelled at, and the whole kitchen goes quiet. Stefan yells at me so often nowadays that not even I notice it that much anymore.

". . . and so I thought I'd ask if you were busy."

Chris—or Topher, actually—is still talking. "Wait, what? You're going where?"

"Yosemite," he repeats patiently. "You know, the national park? I wondered if you wanted to go over break."

"Oh." I give up on finding my highlighter and frown. "Thanks, but I'm going to be busy."

"Right." Topher is deflated. "You're going to Santa Cruz with everyone else."

I blink. Since when do I hang out with "everyone else"? "Nope. Mom's making me check out internships."

"Oh!" Christopher grins. "Interning. Always a good plan."

"Yeah. Lovely. I'd rather go to Yosemite."

"Really?" Chris's, no, Topher's carefully crafted cool wavers. Something sparks in his eyes. "You're serious?"

I notice with relief that Ms. Dunston has set down her coffee cup. "Uh, yeah, Yosemite's great, Chris. Have fun. Look, class is starting, so . . ."

"I'll talk to you after school," Chris says immediately, digging his cell phone out of his pocket. He flips it open importantly. "Your digits?"

How very Topher. I sigh noisily. "Um, your mom has it, right? I mean, it's the same number I've had since the fourth grade, *Chris*." No way does he need my cell number.

Chris sighs and flips closed his phone. I give a barracuda smile. "Sorry, um, *Topher*."

Chris/Topher looks resigned. "Never mind. Nobody remembers. Anyway, I'll call you."

"Whatever . . . ," I say, and shoo him toward his seat.

The sad thing is that Christopher Haines is the one to point out that something big is going on. When I actually take a listen to my classmates, I realize that people are excited about spring break. There are people going to Santa Cruz for a massive house party the first few days, and it hits me that if Sim were here, this is the kind of thing he'd be all over. He'd know the details, and he'd probably be going, and I could be assured of knowing all the dirt that went on there. It would be almost as good as going.

Study hall is full of people whispering, eating, laughing, text-messaging, passing notes, sleeping, and slumping with earphones in their ears. Except for the stoners spacing out and the three people actually studying, everyone else is interacting and interested in each other. It hits me how much of an outsider I am. Sim was into everything, and I've spent my time just watching, looking at the action. Even now, he's off having an adventure, and I'm home waiting for him to at least send a postcard and tell me what's up. And what makes it worse? It's my own choice.

*   *   *

Throughout European history, every time Mr. Fritz walks near my desk, I snap to attention as if I've just wakened out of sleep. Are the Kellers right? Will Sim be showing up somewhere during spring break to reconnect with his friends? Am I one of the ones who will hear from him? What if he's going to be at this big house party in Santa Cruz? Wouldn't he call?

Maybe not. Maybe he's really all the way in Alaska by now.

I pick up my pen and doodle a few notes, wishing Chris Haines hadn't even told me about the house party. I mean, how does *Christopher* know anything, anyway? It's not like getting busted at Sim's party has made him popular, is it? He's as vanilla-plain boring as I am. Chris has always been kind of on the edges of Sim's and my friends, and he's always wanted to hang out with me. With us. Honestly, when he got in trouble at Sim's party, it was probably because he was just there, not because he was involved in anything. Chris probably only found out about the house party lurking on somebody's blog, not because anyone invited him. I mean, people would think to invite me before they invited him, right?

The thought is so petty it makes goose bumps stand up on my arms. My head hits my desk with a thud. I am jealous of Christopher Haines. I am *brain-dead*. It's official.

"Reason, thought the sages of the eighteenth century,

would cure fear, superstition, and prejudice, and in the case of Ben Franklin, it was hoped that it would even conquer death." Mr. Fritz is standing behind me. I get a tighter grip on my pen and frown, trying to look studious and attentive.

"But there was only so much that reason could do. There is a difference between Enlightenment and the enlightened age. And who said that, Elaine?"

"Uhh . . . Immanuel Kant?"

"Are you asking us or telling us, Ms. Seifert?"

Sigh. "Telling you, Mr. Fritz."

"Excellent. So, Immanuel Kant, insofar as it could be said that any of the social engineers of the Enlightenment in the new Europe had a common goal . . ."

Mom's upstairs when I come home, on the phone with Pia or somebody, and I breathe out a sigh of relief. I go straight into the kitchen, washing my hands and tying on my apron. I can't remember the last time I got in here and did anything. Saint Julia has probably forsaken me. Since Sim's been gone, there's been nobody to eat my experiments. I haven't baked for Vocal Jazz or added to my recipe notebooks for weeks. And since Mom's always dragging me to the restaurant in the afternoons, I don't make my own dinner now, and we usually eat something there. I miss cooking for *me.*

Banging around with the pots and pans and the food processor, getting out the good knives, and hunting around to see what's new in the cellar drawer is satisfying, and soon I'm humming along. Mom comes down after a while and leans against the counter watching as I brown the hamburger rolls in the broiler for our hummus burgers and grill some extra onions and mushrooms to go with the tahini sauce.

"Had a good day?" she asks finally.

"It was fine," I say, trying to figure out if the pineapple salsa in the fridge would go with the burgers. I decide no and opt for tomatoes and avocado instead.

"The new menu got reviewed in the *Metro*," Mom offers after a small silence, and I look up at her. She's still wearing her loose cotton work clothes and looks tired.

"Yeah? How'd it go?" My mother asks me every day how my day went, and I don't often ask her anything about hers. I feel a little sliver of guilt.

"It was a really solid review, a really good one. Pia thinks that will start to show in our numbers."

"Cool." I smile at Mom so she knows I really mean it. "Good for you."

Mom pulls out a stool and motions for my tomatoes. I slide her a cutting board and a knife so she can begin slicing.

"Actually, I wanted to talk to you about this. It poses a

little bit of a problem for you and me," Mom continues. "One good review usually means that we'll be reviewed by others—some food magazines, larger local papers, that kind of thing. Things are really starting to change for us now. I feel like I need to get more involved with the restaurant. I may not be able to spend much time finding an internship for you."

I shrug. "Okay."

Mom looks unhappy. "Elaine, I'm really going to need you to follow through on this one for yourself. The way things are going—we're going to seriously need to look at hiring another manager, a real one. I've taken human resources classes, but really—this is all over my head. If we're going to be a success—a real success—it's time to take some big steps." Mom's shoulders seem to slump a little beneath the weight of her words.

"Oh." I wonder if any other response is required.

"Well, don't sound so broken up about it." Mom straightens and rubs a hand over her face and sighs. "You're going to find an internship and let me know. And we're still going to take time to do something together over your spring break, even if it's just a day trip."

The phone rings, saving me from having to defend my lack of enthusiasm. Mom wipes her hands quickly and snags the cordless from the cradle on the kitchen counter.

"Vivianne Seifert.

"Oh, Ana, hi!"

Mom's face lights up and her voice gets louder in that happy way I haven't heard in ages. She picks up the knife again and cocks her head to hold the phone against her ear with her shoulder.

"No, we've been fine! Thank you! It *was* a good review, wasn't it? Pia and I are really thrilled."

I kind of tune out as Mom keeps talking, slicing tomatoes deftly while she chuckles. I wonder if there's a way to talk Mom into going to Santa Cruz. Maybe I can tell her something about seeing UC Santa Cruz. It'd be educational, after all.

Mom's been breathing down my neck so much I just need to get away. I wonder if this is how Sim felt all the time while he was here. Though if it weren't for him, Mom and I wouldn't have this tension between us at all.

As soon as I think the thought, I feel guilty. It might not be true. Maybe if it hadn't been Simeon, something else would have pushed us in different directions. After all, people grow up. . . .

Mom's still talking, but she looks up at me, her brows quirked into a pantomime of surprise. "Really? She didn't say. . . ." She slices the last tomato, then sets down the knife, holding out her hand to stop me from leaving. I wait, fiddling with my apron strings.

"Ana, that's really gracious of you, but we just couldn't. We . . ." A long pause. "No! No, of course not. No, it's not that at all. Well . . . Well, if you're sure it'll be no bother. . . . No, it sounds like it would be really wonderful. All right, let me look at my calendar, and I'll give you a call tomorrow. And, Ana, thank you. I appreciate this so much. It'll be nice to catch up with you and Kevin."

I give Mom a curious glance and lean against the counter as she hangs up. "Kevin who?"

Mom gives me a bemused look. "Kevin Haines. That was Ana."

"Haines?" A terrible suspicion clenches my stomach.

"She and Kevin are going up to their cabin at Yosemite and they invited us up. You know, I remember the year they bought that thing! You and Chris were just—"

I am so far beyond horrified that I can hardly even form the words to interrupt. "Christopher *Haines?* Mom, we're not going, are we?"

My mother gives me a look.

"Mo-*om!*" I know before the word is out how middle school I sound, but I can't help it. This is more than I can take.

"Mom, no. I don't want to spend my whole vacation with Christopher Haines!"

My mother's eyes narrow. "I, I, I, and me, me, me is all I hear from you these days. You're not the only one in this family, Lainey."

I sigh and prepare for a long lecture. "Well, I'm *sorry.* Mrs. Haines is nice, but Chris is kind of a dork. What am I supposed to do with him for a whole week?"

My mother shakes her head, closing her eyes. She must be more tired than I thought. "Tell me, Lainey. Has this boy who's such a 'dork' got parents saying they're going to sue me? Does he lie to them? Has he run away from home?"

Shocked, I suck in a breath through my teeth. "Mom! That's not fair. Chris isn't Sim! And anyway, it's only been one time something like that has happened with Simeon, once."

"Elaine, all it takes is once." My mother's voice is clipped.

"What's that supposed to mean?" Tension crowds my stomach.

My mother cocks her head. "Did you think I didn't listen to what you said? Did you think I wouldn't look at my bank records, at the dates? You haven't been totally straight about what went on with Simeon, Elaine, and I've been waiting and hoping, but . . ." She shrugs.

"Mom—" My stomach clamps with dread. "Wait. Let me—"

"You said you didn't give Simeon 'much' money, and I find a five-hundred-dollar cash withdrawal from my account. . . ."

"But, Mom, that was just—"

"You *said* he came to this house for dinner on Friday, but you made him sandwiches on the rolls I brought home from the restaurant well after you were in bed asleep on Friday night."

"Mom, I can explain—"

"You *said* you don't know where he went, and you know what, Laine? I don't believe you. I've always been able to trust you before this, and now that I've found that I can't—well, you can look forward to me being a whole lot more skeptical of what you *say*, Miss It-only-happened-one-time. Once is enough to break a trust." My mother sets down the knife firmly.

"Mom." I'm groping for words. "This . . . it isn't a big deal! That was my money from Grandma Muriel. You said that. And anyway . . . I never meant to lie to you."

"Oh no, of course not," Mom says acidly. "But you opened your mouth and did it anyway, didn't you?"

EAST-WEST HUMMUS BURGERS

- 1/2 LARGE ONION, FINELY DICED
- 1-1/4 C. VEGETABLE STOCK
- 1 C. COARSE BULGUR WHEAT OR QUICK-COOK ROLLED OATS
- 2 (15 OZ.) CANS CHICKPEAS (GARBANZOS), DRAINED AND RINSED
- 2 TSP. EACH CORIANDER SEED AND CUMIN
- PINCH KOSHER SALT
- 6 TSP. FRESH PARSLEY, CHOPPED (TRY CILANTRO!)

OPTIONAL: 1 EGG TO BIND

1/4 C. GRATED MOZZARELLA OR PARMESAN, FOR FLAVOR

ADD ONIONS INTO A 3-QUART SAUCEPAN WITH THE VEGETABLE STOCK AND BRING TO A SIMMER. ADD BULGUR AND CHICKPEAS AND STIR UNTIL COMBINED. TURN OFF HEAT, COVER, AND LET STAND 15 MINUTES OR UNTIL ALL LIQUID IS ABSORBED.

IN A SMALL, DRY SAUCE PAN, ROAST CUMIN AND CORIANDER SEEDS OVER MEDIUM HEAT, SHAKING THE PAN OFTEN. DRY ROAST THEM UNTIL YOU CAN SMELL THEM, AND THEY TURN SLIGHTLY BROWN, WHICH WILL TAKE ABOUT TWO MINUTES. DON'T BURN THEM! SHAKE SEEDS INTO A COFFEE GRINDER OR SPICE MILL TO GRIND THEM, THEN ADD TO CHICKPEA AND BULGUR MIX.

REMOVE   ADD SALT.
⌄POT FROM HEAT AND⌄ WITH A POTATO MASHER OR SPOON BACK,
MASH INGREDIENTS TOGETHER, MAKING SURE ALL CHICKPEAS GET
SMASHED. ADD CHOPPED PARSLEY AND CHEESE OR 1 EGG AS AN OPTION.
FORM INTO 4 PATTIES. LIGHTLY COAT A 10-INCH NONSTICK PAN
WITH COOKING SPRAY AND TURN HEAT TO MEDIUM. PLACE
ALL BURGERS IN PAN WHEN HOT AND COOK 2 TO 3 MINUTES
PER SIDE OR UNTIL HEATED THROUGH AND GOLDEN.

* * TRY TACO SEASONING IN THE MIX OR ZAATAR
      SPICE FOR A MORE MEDITERRANEAN / MOROCCAN FLAVOR.

* * SERVE WITH GRILLED PORTABELLA MUSHROOMS OR TAHINI
      SAUCE AND REGULAR BURGER FIXINGS. LOTS OF GRILLED
      RED ONIONS ARE PRIMO! REALLY GOOD WITH A MANGO
      LASSI ON THE SIDE!

14

It isn't until we're behind the first motor home of the day that I realize just how long this trip is going to take. We're lucky Christopher Haines is driving down with us even though he's been a total suck-up to Mom. At least he's a suck-up who knows the way to a house with a decent bathroom.

Mom's face scrunches up in impatience as we inch up the serpentine roads, her fingers drumming on the steering wheel.

"Thank goodness for passing lanes," she mutters as we accelerate past the bulky vehicle. We made a wrong turn somewhere, and now we're backtracking through the valley floor. We slowly drive past campsites and cinder block bathrooms, skirting cyclists and hikers in an overabundance of plaid.

I shrug and look out the window again. The boulders

are immense, making ants of those of us on the road with their incredible height. Wide-bottomed trees snuggle against the thin ribbon of road, and grass and wildflowers struggle to cover every available growing surface. Farther along, the sky seems almost within reach of the massive woods.

"Just look at those trees," Mom sighs.

"They're giant sequoias," Chris says, well into his tour-guide act.

"So were you a Cub Scout or what?" I ask.

Chris laughs uncomfortably. "No."

The little silence that follows makes me happy, even though I know my mother is glaring at me in the rearview mirror. I deliberately lean toward the window and look up. We're dwarfed by dramatic granite cliffs and looming chains of snow-capped mountains. It's actually gorgeous out here.

"So, Chris? What are those little brown metal boxes? Do they recycle up here?" Mom points out the window.

Chris looks over his sunglasses. "They're bear boxes."

Mom gives a theatrical shudder. "Bear boxes? There are bears?"

I roll my eyes at Mom's theatrical shivers. "Well, we're in the woods."

Chris grins. "Pretty much anything will get into your food—or your car—if you leave it out, and nothing stops a bear from eating something unless he can't get to it."

"It's not like that's an issue since we're staying in a *cabin*." I don't address my comment to anyone in particular, but my mother knows I'm talking to her.

"Well, it's just an issue when you put out garbage," Chris corrects me. "But the Dumpsters are pretty far from the cabins, and they lock too." He turns back to Mom.

"Bears aren't really a problem, Mrs. Seifert. I've seen a couple of bears up here before, and mostly they're pretty nonaggressive."

Whatever. I roll down the window and smell the air, tinged with pine and wood smoke. When we were packing, Mom left a box on the counter for any seasonings and specialty items from the kitchen she thought I'd want, since cooking in the back of beyond is bound to be a little limited. As I look at the long stretches of woods and quaint A-frames, I wish I'd packed more than fresh herbs and dried spices. I feel like I should've brought the whole refrigerator. Plus pots.

"Tent-cabins are what they call those little huts." Chris points out a distant campsite from his post in the front passenger seat. "They've got outlets. You can bring a heater." Mom makes some agreeable noises about tents and camping in general, like she's an expert, and I shake my head in disbelief. Chris offered to sit in back when we got started, but Mom told him he'd better navigate, and then she proceeded to yak for three hours. It's taking forever to get to the cabin. Between tourists braking abruptly and pulling over to snap pictures of the gushing waterfalls, ground squirrels, tall trees, and patches of snow in the woods and Mom not actually listening to Chris when he tells her to turn, I'm going insane. Plus, Mom's been doing this subtle interrogation thing the entire drive, asking Chris about his grades, his friends, and his college choices, which I think is pointless. After this long cooped up in the car, even if he were someone interesting, he'd be working my last nerve. He's just too patient, and he and Mom are having too much fun.

"The old Wawona Hotel is just off that way," Chris continues, pointing. "They've got a Pioneer Center or something around there too, you know, horses and buggies and that kind of thing."

"Oh, Lainey should like that," Mom says brightly, her eyes checking for my reaction in her mirror.

Chris laughs. "Yeah, it was pretty good when I was about eight or nine."

"Oh." Mom smiles again. "Well, I'm looking forward to seeing it anyway."

He shrugs. "There's a nice golf course out there, uh, the Mariposa Grove, and . . . the Wawona has a decent restaurant. Maybe you'd like to go, huh, Lainey? You think?"

The thin bubble of personal space I'd constructed

between the front and back seats pops abruptly. *What? Did he just ask me out? Is he kidding me?* "I didn't bring any clothes. . . . Actually, I thought I'd . . . um . . . cook something."

"Lainey," Mom chides, "where's your sense of fun? That place is a national landmark, and they've got a world-famous chef!"

"She's just not in vacation mode yet," Chris says agreeably.

"What*ever*," I mutter.

"You can cook us something tonight," Mom says, trying to sound placating. I sigh and look out the window.

"It's a nice place," Chris says, turning around. He seems very intent. "You'd like it. We should go."

I blink at him. He's practically ordering me to go out with him.

"Chris . . ."

"Mom and Dad are having some friends of theirs over tomorrow night," Chris adds. "It's a card party. It'll be more fun to go out. You'll thank me." He shrugs.

"Fine." I have no idea why he thinks his company is preferable to his parents', but I'll say just about anything at this point to get him to turn around and leave me alone already.

The cabin isn't as posh-looking as I expected, at least from the outside. It's old and comfortable, an A-frame

203

nestled beneath tall trees with dark-stained redwood decks and leaf litter on the stairs. There's a sweet, piney smell in the air. It's quiet, except for the sounds filtering from the cabin across the street, which is filled with hyperactive adults running up and down the stairs, unloading their SUV.

Mr. and Mrs. Haines meet us at the door, looking relaxed and happy. When I see Mr. Haines, I realize how much Christopher takes after his mom, who shares his olive coloring, broad shoulders, and dark wavy hair. Mrs. Haines is wearing a bright floral wrap skirt, T-shirt, and clogs, and I feel sweaty and overdressed in my jeans and hoodie. Mr. Haines looks like a Clark Kent–type dad, mild-mannered, tall, and soft-spoken, wearing rimless glasses. His silvery hair is cropped military short, in contrast to Chris's twisty mop.

"Welcome! We're so glad you could make it!" Mrs. Haines says, enveloping Mom in a big hug. As always, she talks a mile a minute, inquires about the drive (*isn't it gorgeous?*), exclaims over the traffic (*it was horrendous!*), thanks Mom for fetching Chris from school, kisses him soundly on the forehead (earning herself a look of mild reproof), and generally makes our appearance a noisy and confusing event. Mr. Haines shakes my hand, takes the box of kitchen stuff we brought from home, and retreats behind the dining room table with a vague smile. He must do that a lot.

"Thanks for inviting us, Mrs. Haines," I mutter dutifully in the limited space between Mom's gushing and Mrs. Haines's welcome.

"Oh, you're grown up now, Elaine—you're old enough now to call me Ana," she insists, squeezing my shoulder with a friendly hand. "We're so glad you're here. But we'll catch up later—Christopher, show them their rooms!"

Mom and Mrs. Haines have chattered away any feeling of awkwardness I might have had about spending time in the cabin. It is clean and comfortable-looking, and the airy rooms make me think of reading quietly during long evenings and getting up early to see the sun. The carpeting upstairs is straight out of the seventies, some kind of brown pile, but it's soft and thick. The walls are a light tan instead of the homestead pine planks I expected, and the bedroom has bunk beds. Mom's right on my heels when Chris shows us where to dump our stuff and points out the bathrooms.

"Do you want the bottom bunk?" Mom asks politely. I shrug. What I really want is for her not to share a room with me, but I can see she's going to, and she's going to be chipper and upbeat and ignore the fact that I'm grumpy and not really speaking to her.

I dump my stuff on the bed and call out to Chris, "So, is there anyplace to get groceries around here?"

"We're mostly stocked." Chris appears in the hallway.

"Mom and Dad usually take care of the shopping on their last day and then buy fresh stuff the next time. Is there anything special you wanted? What do you want to cook?"

"Whatever." I shrug, suddenly feeling tired.

"Don't you usually cook at home?" Chris wants to know.

"Well . . ."

"Oh, Lainey, don't be modest! This girl has won contests." My mother comes out of the room and places a hand lightly on my shoulder. "Why don't you two go in the kitchen and see what you need? I saw a grocery store on the way up if you want anything more."

If I wanted to cook before, I fully don't want to now. I turn around and give her a look.

"Lainey . . . go. Show your stuff, huh?" Mom pushes me toward the stairs.

Gritting my teeth, I go down to the main level. Mrs. Haines—Ana—has put out soda and a plate of vegetables, dip, and chips on the counter, with paper plates for us to help ourselves. The pantry is open. Mrs. Haines looks like she's taking inventory, and on the counter are boxes of breakfast cereal and biscuit mix, cans of beans, boxes of pasta, and frozen foods. Mrs. Haines straightens from putting something into a cabinet.

"Are you guys hungry yet? I was going to start dinner, but I haven't been shopping yet, and I wasn't sure what you wanted. . . . Lainey, what do you like to eat? Shall we order pizza? Curry Village actually has a place where we can pick some up, or get burgers, or—"

"Lainey's cooking," Chris announces. He seats himself on a bar stool. "She's an amazing baker; she always brings stuff to Vocal Jazz—you've got to taste something of hers."

Chris makes it sound like I came just for the sole purpose of cooking a meal for him. "No! I don't have to! I just thought—"

Ana interrupts with great enthusiasm. "Marvelous! Christopher, stay in the kitchen and pick up some pointers from this, huh? You'll be cooking for yourself when you go away to college next year."

I am the focus of three pairs of interested eyes as the Haines family lines up on the other side of the bar and watches my progress. I want a cooking show someday, but this studio audience is way too close. If I were at home, this would be a piece of cake. *Cake* . . . I see a box of mix. But we can't have that for dinner. "Um . . ."

Without my notebooks, I'm lost. This is my vacation. I wasn't planning on showing off for anyone but myself.

"Well . . ." My mind is gibbering as I survey my domain. Where's Saint Julia when I need her? The kitchen is huge, with a gas range, a double oven, what looks like some kind of grill backed by a brick wall, and lots and lots of pine drawers and cabinets.

"Uh . . ." I'm rescued by the sight of a bag of apples. "If you have an apple corer . . ."

Ana frowns. "Well . . . no. But will a knife . . . ?"

"No problem," I say quickly, switching gears from the baked apple idea I was going to use. "Christopher, if you could slice some apples . . ."

"Apple pie?" he asks shrewdly.

No dice, smart guy. I can't stand making pastry crusts. "Crumble."

"Huh." Chris sounds mystified.

The quick dessert is already in my head, but with five people, I've got to make something else reasonably speedy and filling. Chris gets busy slicing the four apples I handed him, and I leave him to his mother's interference ("Thinner, honey. She said 'thin.'") and ponder the main event. I cast around, desperately looking at the groceries on the counter. Mom and I usually have fresh food around the house, but the canned beans and chicken broth give me an idea. If only there's some frozen corn. . . . I grimace when I find canned, but it's better than nothing.

"Chowder," I mutter. What will I need? I strain to recall an episode of a Jacques Pépin cooking show. Then Mr. Haines brings over the box of ingredients from home, and I take a deep breath with relief. My cilantro is a frothy green flag, waving me onward. I fill a glass with water and stuff the herb into it after snipping off the stems. This way, it will be fresh for a while longer.

"Need any help?" Mom appears at my side, beaming smugly.

I ignore her expression. "Menu suggestions," I say, feeling overwhelmed. "I'm thinking a corn chowder with maybe some muffins?"

"Oh, I have a mix," Ana interjects. "I found one in the back of the pantry."

My mother gives me a level look, and I return it. *Mix.* We never use mix. That's blasphemy at our house. But it's better than nothing by far. "Thank you," I say fervently. I turn to my mother.

"Do you think there's hominy at the store?"

"Hominy? Well, I'll look." Mom purses her lips doubtfully. "If not, it'll be fine without, won't it?"

I nod. I prefer to have everything I need when I cook, but you can't think of everything.

"If you're going to the store, I'll go with you, Vivi," Ana announces. "Loren's coming down Tuesday night— I think we'll need a little more food. At least some frozen pizza. Loren eats like a sumo wrestler. You know that boy tries to live solely on ramen noodles at school?"

"Apples are done," Chris announces.

"Great. You guys have a muffin tin?"

"Uh . . ." Chris starts slamming cupboards. "Think so . . ."

"Okay. Could you oil it and then crush me a package of graham crackers?"

Chris looks up. "Graham crackers?"

"Yep. All the way into crumbs, please."

"What are you doing with graham crackers?"

I wish I knew. "A good sous-chef follows directions, Chris."

"Right." Chris grins. "I can do that."

I give him a panicky little smile as I try to think of what to do next.

At least being put on the spot like this has pushed everything else out of my head. Mr. Haines is still watching me cook and offers to fill the muffin tin when I get the batter stirred. I've added some of the canned corn, drained, a can of chopped chilies, and some sliced, jalapeño-stuffed green martini olives to the mix to make it seem less commercial. Mr. Haines works with great concentration, filling each indentation to an exact depth in spite of the chunky texture of the batter by shaking the pan and occasionally smacking it on the surface of the counter to remove any air pockets. After a particularly loud slam against the counter, Chris and I share a glance of fleeting amusement. Mr. Haines carries on, carefully filling and leveling each muffin. I almost feel a little guilty that all we're going to do is turn out his works of art and eat them.

The Haineses' kitchen is all about canned, jarred, and boxed items, and it takes a while to find what I need. Chopped garlic is in a jar in the fridge, and I add a teaspoon of its pungent paste to about two tablespoons of olive oil in a deep saucepan. I add a chopped onion and a few scallions from home, wishing I'd packed more.

I don't find the electric can opener until I've already opened a can of tomatoes with a manual opener and added them and about a half cup of salsa verde that I found in the back of the fridge, looking a little old but none the worse for wear. I open two cartons of vegetable broth I brought from home and measure four cups into the pot.

Both Mr. Haines and Chris look startled when I add a half teaspoon of cinnamon to the soup. I tense, not realizing that they were still watching me so closely. But they are my studio audience, after all.

"It's good," I promise them. "Really." Aware of their dubious looks, I pull out my mortar and pestle and grind up about two teaspoons of cumin seeds. A pinch of thyme adds even more complexity to the dish. As soon as Mom gets back, I'll add the canned hominy (may she please find some, oh please, please), chop the cilantro, and add the canned corn. I wish we had fresh. An investigation of the freezer doesn't turn up any, but I do find some frozen fruit, a little treasure I keep in mind for later.

I assemble the dessert topping, using Chris's crushed graham crackers seasoned with freshly ground nutmeg, two tablespoons of butter, two tablespoons of water, and a few spritzes of butter-flavored nonstick spray.

"Why do you use butter and butter spray both?" Mr. Haines asks, looking up from his muffin construction.

"Oh! Well, to start with, it's lower fat," I blurt in my best cooking show voice, and then freeze. *Nice one, Lainey.* My neck heats in shame.

"Good to know." Mr. Haines nods. Chris flicks me a glance but doesn't comment.

I feel like an idiot. Unnerved, I go for another rummage in the freezer. Finding frozen peaches makes my embarrassment seem less important. I drag them out gleefully, not even allowing the words *enhanced with natural flavors* (who knows what those are?) to dim my happiness. The addition of peaches will make the crumble phenomenal.

Mr. Haines is taking the muffins out when Mom and Ana get back almost an hour later. Mom hands me a big bag of frozen corn with a look of restrained triumph.

Thank goodness. "Oh! Great. Did you find . . . ?"

Mom hands me a can with Spanish and English labeling, and I relax. "Hominy. Perfect."

I dump in the hominy and get Chris started alternating the apples on the bottom of the graham cracker crust with a layer of peaches atop them. The peaches are frozen, but he and Mr. Haines eat more than a couple before the job gets done. Ana contributes a cup of her high-fiber breakfast cereal, crushed, which I add to a cup of plain rolled oats moistened with milk and a half cup of sugar to make the paste, which will bake into a crunchy topping for the fruit.

Chris eyes the chunky concoction over the fruit. "You got ice cream, right, Mom?"

"I did," Ana says.

"We even got some of the kind you like," Mom tells me, and I smile sheepishly.

"You didn't have to do that," I mutter. Mom shrugs and smiles. In spite of myself, I feel a little warmer toward her right now. It's true she's being unreasonable about everything and dragging me on this stupid vacation, but it's hard to carry a grudge against someone who buys you a pricey little pint of soy ice cream out in the boonies.

The muffins are fragrant and golden brown. The soup is mildly spicy and delicious, the savory cilantro and juicy frozen corn a flavorful last-minute addition. The hominy is bland and creamy, the perfect comfort food. There is a complimentary silence as the first bites are taken.

"Nice job. You outdid yourself," Mom murmurs.

"Elaine, this is amazing," Ana gushes. "You have got to teach Christopher to cook!"

Chris gives them a disgusted look, and his parents share a laugh at his expense. Then Ana launches into a story about the first time she experienced hominy grits, somewhere in Charleston, South Carolina. Mr. Haines counters with an explanation of what hominy is and how it is made. I make short work of a muffin (it's decent, even for a mix) as he explains how the early Americans used a samp mill to grind the grains and an ash hopper to rinse wood ashes and create the lye, which was used to soften the tough outer kernel of corn. As Mr. Haines talks, Chris gives me a sideways glance, his expression measuring, but I barely notice him. Mr. Haines, once he finally starts to talk, is really interesting.

"Are you a history teacher?" I ask him.

He smiles, suddenly awkward again, and I see a quick shadow of a vulnerable Chris in his expression. "Nope. Engineer."

"He watches cooking shows," Ana explains fondly, giving his hand a squeeze.

A kindred spirit!

Everyone makes a big fuss over the soup, but dessert is a hit I didn't expect. The raisins in Ana's cereal got plumped up with the peach juice and are exclamation points of flavor throughout the chewy, crunchy topping.

The rich sweetness of the peaches is contrasted with the more-tart flavor of the apples. Chris smothers his serving in ice cream, then offers a scoop to me.

"Oh, no thanks," I say. I've eaten more than I should have.

"It's good," Chris coaxes. "It's vanilla bean."

"Well, okay," I agree awkwardly, and scrape out about a teaspoonful from the scoop. He's incredulous but puts the scoop back into the carton and passes it along the table.

Everyone is clearing the table, groaning from fullness. Ana tells me I should sit and not do anything, but I get up good-naturedly and take my plate to the dishwasher. Christopher is bagging the leftover raw vegetables.

"Hey, Lainey. You're not . . . on a diet or something, are you?"

"Christopher Sebastian Haines," says Ana, catching his comment. "Really!"

"No, I was just saying." Chris ducks his head, embarrassed. "You shouldn't be. I mean, if you are. You look, uh, fine. I mean, okay. You know, good."

My skin tightens with embarrassed heat as blood rushes to my face and neck. For a moment, I'm silenced by disbelief. Christopher Haines is hitting on me? My life has reached a new low. "Um . . . thanks." I look around uncomfortably. "I . . . um, I'm going for a walk."

"Oh, Christopher, you should go with her. Walk down with her to the river. If you're quiet out there, you might see some wildlife."

"If we're that still, we're going to come back with malaria from mosquito bites," Chris mutters.

My mother says, "Long pants, long sleeves, and repellent. Remember the West Nile."

"Watch out for the long grass," Mr. Haines says mildly.

The grass? I shoot Chris a bewildered look.

"Deer ticks," he says pleasantly. "They hang on to the tips of long grass blades and then jump on you when they feel your body heat. They give you Lyme disease."

I flinch. Maybe I don't want to go outside.

This far from home, the light seems to linger longer. The sun is filtering crookedly through the trees as we walk down the front stairs and away from the house. I wish Chris weren't with me. Everything he says makes me feel uncomfortable, and he keeps on talking to fill the silence. I'm horrified by what he said. Does he really think I look "good," or was that just him being polite? I'm even more horrified that I care.

"Lainey. Wait up," Chris orders. I'd started away from him at a brisk walk, and I'm not ready to slow down.

"Keep up," I call over my shoulder, and keep going. I'm aware I'm being difficult but don't know what else to do. My plan for this vacation was not to spend moonlit nights walking by the river with Christopher Haines.

Chris closes the distance between us easily. "Wait. I'm supposed to be showing you the wildlife. Slow down."

"Yeah? Well, I'm not sure I want to find it." I keep striding. I hear his shoes crunch the pine needles on the road as he jogs to catch up.

There's a silence as he catches up and walks at a stiff-legged lope to match my pace. I'm practically running just to keep him from walking right next to me. Finally, he shoves his hands in his jacket pockets and stops. "Lainey . . . ," he sighs. "What did I ever do to you?"

Oh *no*. I slow to a guilty walk, my face flaming. "Chris—"

Chris interrupts. "Never mind. Look, I just was going to say I was glad you guys came, that's all. I wasn't looking forward to just hanging with my folks all week, and Loren's probably bringing friends down too, so I'm glad you're here. That's all I was going to say."

I stop in the middle of the path, feeling a moth blunder into my head. "Yeah, thanks, Ch . . . Topher. It was cool of your parents to invite us. I'm . . . It'll be fun."

"Yeah?" Chris brightens visibly; even in the darkness I can see him standing up taller, straighter. My words making such a huge difference to him immediately depresses me.

"Let's walk." I start off again.

We move out of the trees and up a little rise where we can better see the sky, which is slate blue with a flaming rosy glow that fades to the palest of pink-washed gold. Chris continues his nature walk, pointing out bats making their graceless flight between the dark sentinels of trees. At least a hundred times I open my mouth to ask him how many badges he got in Cub Scouts or whatever, but I stop myself. He's trying to be nice. I sigh and nod like I actually care.

A whine in my ear alerts us to mosquitoes, and we hurry back to the house, pulling our sweatshirts up around our necks. We're almost to the door when Christopher, kicking a pinecone, says, "So . . . you and Keller still going out?"

What? I stumble on something invisible, then recover. "Who even said we were?"

PEACH APPLE CRISP

DESSERT RECIPE : IN PROGRESS !!

1 - 10 oz. BAG OF FROZEN PEACHES

2 MEDIUM APPLES , TART, PEELED, SLICED

1/2 TSP. VANILLA EXTRACT

1/4 TSP. GROUND CINNAMON

1/4 TSP. NUTMEG

3/4 C. + 3 TBSP. ALL PURPOSE FLOUR
     (WHATEVER FLOUR IS AVAILABLE WILL WORK)

1/4 C. BROWN SUGAR, PACKED (RAW SUGAR WORKS ALSO,
     BUT ALSO ADD 1 TBSP. MOLASSES)

3 TBSP, BUTTER CHILLED

PREHEAT OVEN TO 350°F. LIGHTLY GREASE 9x9x2 INCH
CASSEROLE DISH. COMBINE PEACHES ,APPLES , VANILLA ,
AND CINNAMON IN A BOWL. TOSS WELL AND SPREAD
EVENLY IN GREASED CASSEROLE DISH. COMBINE NUTMEG, FLOUR,
AND SUGAR IN SMALL BOWL. CUT IN BUTTER WITH
TWO KNIVES UNTIL THE MIXTURE RESEMBLES COARSE MEAL.
SPRINKLE FLOUR MIXTURE EVENLY OVER FRUIT.

BAKE UNTIL LIGHTLY BROWNED AND BUBBLY, ABOUT
20 MINUTES

* * CANNED PEARS DON'T WORK WELL FOR THIS, BUT FRESH PEARS DO AND ~~FRESH~~ PEACHES — DEFINITELY! IF USING FRESH PEACHES, USE 5 (LARGE) AND SKIP THE APPLES. IF USING FRESH PEARS, SKIN THEM. CANNED PEACHES TASTE... LIKE CANS. FROZEN FRUIT, ANY KIND = BETTER.

15

"What are you up to, Laine?"

Mom finds me atop my bunk late in the afternoon, digging in my bag for my headphones. It's been a strangely quiet day. Mr. Haines went fishing, and Topher slept until almost noon. Mom and I had the kitchen to ourselves and, at the lazy urging of Ana, made loads of blueberry crêpes for a late brunch. We started out with a pancake mix but with the berries I found in the freezer made a passable compote, so it wasn't all that bad. Still, I made a note to bring along a real crêpe recipe next time I go on vacation.

I shrug irritably, flinging things out of my bag on my quest now for batteries. "Topher wants me to go out with him to that hotel."

"Sounds like fun," my mother says noncommittally, smiling.

I make an impatient noise. "Well, then *you* go. I can't

see the attraction." I find the batteries and bend my nail trying to open the back of my MP3 player.

Last night, I wanted to talk about Simeon for the rest of the evening. I wanted to *grill* Topher on everything that happened at that party. I wanted to know who else was there and what else was said. Instead, as soon as we walked into the house, Mom and Ana dragged us into playing canasta with them, and then we stayed up late watching movies. This afternoon Topher stuck a note under my door, reminding me about dinner at the hotel again. He seems to think I came on this trip to hang out with him.

"Elaine." Mom's voice is sharp. "I hope you're not being rude to that boy."

"No, I'm not." I'm exasperated, wishing my mother didn't always think the absolute worst of me. "Mom, even *you* can't think that just because I'm here, I have to go out with him."

Mom laughs dryly. "No, I don't think that, but there's such a thing as courtesy, Elaine, and I expect you to show you have at least a nodding acquaintance with that."

"I know how to be courteous," I mutter grouchily. I slam my headphones back into my bag. "And anyway, I hear the restaurant does a world-class steak!"

Mom sighs and ignores my sarcasm. "Have fun," she

says tiredly. "I'm going to find somewhere my cell phone will work and touch base with Pia. Last I heard from her, we were having some trouble with one of our distributors, and the thermocouple in one of the ovens went out last night during service."

I immediately feel guilty. "Mom, you're *supposed* to be on vacation, you know."

"I know. So, go and have dessert for me tonight, okay? And . . . be nice to Topher. He really is such a nice boy, Laine. Remember what I said about being open to new experiences?"

I grit my teeth. I should have known better than to feel sorry for my mother, who is happiest when she is arranging everything, including my social life.

When I'm finally dressed, I walk down the stairs into the middle of another one of Ana's effusive welcomes. Loren Haines is a taller, heavier version of his brother, and it's almost eerie looking at him as he shakes my hand.

"Nice to meet another one of Topher's friends," Loren says, but he's loud and friendly like Ana, and so it doesn't come out sounding like he means anything more than what he says.

"Loren's only here to drop off his laundry," Ana announces dryly, shaking her head. "He's off to see his friends, even though he just got here."

"I'll be here for dinner, Ma," Loren protests. "The party's not till late."

Ana rolls her eyes and motions toward her other son. "Topher, you two had better get going."

Topher's just wearing a striped shirt and jeans, but I feel a little underdressed. The nicest thing I brought is a V-necked pink sweater, which looks only so-so with a gray T-shirt and short denim skirt underneath. If I had known I was supposed to pack something other than granola-girl gear, I might have come up with something better.

"Does this look okay?" I mutter to Topher. My hair is as shiny as I could make it, and I'm wearing lip gloss and Mom's silver filigreed hoops.

There is surprise, then confirmation in Topher's smile. "Yeah."

"You two go and have a good time," Ana encourages us warmly, beaming, and I see Mr. Haines give Topher's shoulder a squeeze and tuck a wad of bills into his shirt pocket. Mom stands by, dimpling, and I have the horrible sense that someone's going to insist on taking pictures pretty soon. Topher must be feeling the too-interested parent vibe too, because he rushes me out of the door as fast as he can.

The hotel itself is a little bit of a distraction. It's old-fashioned enough that the horse and buggy sitting in front doesn't look out of place. A fountain sunk into the lawn blows crystal drops of water into the air. The long, broad porches that surround the hotel look like they've seen the likes of Mark Twain and John Muir relaxing in their shadowy depths.

I find myself looking around, derailed, for the moment, from anything but the scenery, but Topher leads the way into the hotel. I feel a twinge of embarrassment the moment we step into the high-ceilinged lobby. Creamy patterned wallpaper and gilt-framed pictures surround antique chairs and other furniture. My already-tight stomach lurches when we enter the hotel dining room. Tiffany-style, painted chandeliers illuminate rows of white-clothed tables. *This* is not a little woodsy lodge with fast food. Topher pulls out one of the tall-backed chairs.

"Oh . . . thanks," I say inadequately. The waitress hands us menus, and Topher orders soda water with lime for both of us. Fancy. I glance around the room and fidget with the napkin in my lap until the waitress goes away.

Topher clears his throat and plays with his fork. There's a weird nervousness to his movements. I'm not sure what to think, and I don't want to focus on Topher right now. I keep looking around. "Those pinecone chandeliers are interesting."

"Sequoia."

"What?"

Topher traces a pattern with his finger. "They're sequoia cones"—Topher gives a vague nod with his chin toward the windows—" 'cause of the giant se-quoias."

"And the difference is . . . ?" I'm just messing with him, but I know it's going to set him on one of his nature rants.

Topher takes a breath. "Well, the difference," he begins, then stops, catching something in my expression. "It's not that big a difference," he sighs, shaking his head. "I know you don't actually care anyway."

I smile. "Not really."

I people-watch for a while, noting aloud that Topher and I are probably the youngest people in the dining room without parents. This is nothing like La Salle: though the servers are nicely dressed, there's definitely a more-casual vibe from the diners, as a family comes in with strollers and shorts.

"Miss?" The waitress interrupts with our drinks. Topher takes his napkin and opens my bottle, then his own. He's being very formal, which makes me want to laugh.

"Christopher, you don't have to keep pretending we're on a date."

Topher flinches. "I'm not."

Oops. "Well, I just mean you're being really nice. You don't . . . have to. I mean . . ."

Topher shrugs and studies his menu. "Do you see anything you want? You can get whatever. Dad gave me enough."

"No!" I give him a horrified look. "Chris, I have money. You're not paying for me."

A shrug. "Whatever."

Uncomfortably, I scan the menu, glancing up periodically to study Chris's face. He didn't really think this was a "going out" kind of dinner, did he? It's all I can do to keep from asking him, which is just as well. He doesn't say anything else until the waitress comes.

We make it through dinner only because there's nothing else to do. Topher orders the flatiron steak, which comes with garlic whipped potatoes and toasted cumin-avocado butter, which on any other day I'd really want to try. I request a bowl of minestrone soup and a house salad, which includes roasted walnuts and cherry tomatoes in a soy ginger vinaigrette. Topher gives me a disbelieving look.

I'm almost too edgy to notice how good the soup tastes, but not quite. I make note of the ingredients, tucking them away in my memory to try out later.

"How's the cumin-avocado sauce?"

"Fine." Topher wipes his mouth and keeps his eyes down.

O-kay. I give up and go back to my minestrone.

The white-aproned waitress returns, perky and smiling. "Did you save room for dessert?"

"No, thank you," I say automatically, glancing across the table at Chris. He's been so silent all evening I thought he'd just want to get away, but he looks irritated. Does he think I'm trying to be cheap? I never get dessert in restaurants anymore, but how can I say that?

"I'll make dessert," I tell him, coming up with the idea suddenly. "When we get back."

The waitress beams. "That sounds like a lovely way to end the evening."

Topher shrugs, blowing out a breath. "Whatever. We'll take the check, please."

The waitress gives a plastic smile and glides away.

Prickling with embarrassment, I stare at Topher. "What's up with you?"

He shrugs.

"No, seriously. What's wrong? You don't want me to make dessert?" I study Topher's face for any sign of amusement, hostility, anything. His pointed chin is set, and his usually cheerful expression, framed by bleached, twisted baby dreadlocks, is cold. He flicks a glance at me, his dark grayish eyes flat.

I realize I have rarely ever really looked at Christopher Haines. There is something shuttered tight in his gaze. He turns away and mutters something.

"What?"

Topher leans forward and speaks slowly, enunciating every word. "I said, this is stupid."

I sit back. "Stupid?"

"Should I say it again?" There is a sullen expression on Topher's face.

I bite my top lip, my toes curling with discomfort. "What—"

"I thought it would make a difference if we weren't at school." Topher's voice is leaden. "Even without everybody else around, you still act like I'm something you stepped in."

"Wait. *Wait.*" This conversation has gotten entirely surreal. "What do you mean?"

Topher looks across the dining room out of the tall windows to the slowly fading light. "You're blowing me off just like you always do. What, now I'm such a freak you can't even eat with me? Whatever."

"Chris . . ." I flail for words. "I don't think anything of you, I swear. I mean . . . I don't think anything bad about you, okay?" I'm feeling panicky. "And . . ."

"Your friend Keller blew me off too." Topher is still talking, watching the candle flickering in the middle of the table. "At his party, I watched him get all messed up, and then, when the cops came, he suddenly remembered my name. He's like, 'Topher, I need a huge favor.' And he gives me this little bag. . . . Then he's all, 'I got your back, man,' and when I get picked up, he gets away clean, but they thought I was dealing." Topher's chin comes up. "It was my own fault. I'm not stupid. I know you don't just 'hold something' for someone and get off scot-free. But I just thought—"

"Chris . . ." My stomach is curdling. I don't want to hear any more.

"It's Topher," he snaps, and I flinch. The waitress chooses that moment to return with the check.

"Have a lovely evening," she chirps artificially, her eyes above our heads, already moving on to the next table.

Topher grabs the bill and reaches for his wallet, his level stare challenging. I don't move. I'm afraid if I reach for my purse, he'll start shouting.

Topher tosses down a few bills and pushes back from the table.

I take a deep breath. "Topher?" I lean forward. "I'm sorry. I didn't know. . . . Look, I'll make it up to you. . . ." I hear the phrase and freeze. Never have the words sounded quite so false. My stomach congeals. I breathe out slowly.

"Actually? I probably won't. That's really just a polite

excuse, isn't it? I don't think there's anything I can do to make up for . . . anything. Will you excuse me?"

The noise of cutlery and polite conversation is drowned out by my choppy breaths as I escape from the dining room. I'm walking as fast as I can, knowing that Topher is probably watching me, knowing that I'm attracting attention from the other hotel patrons. I need some air.

Julia Child didn't cry when her soufflé collapsed on national television. I can't cry. Not here in the lobby of this gracious hotel full of Victorian antiques. I don't have any tissue.

Outside, the wind is ruffling the tops of the trees, and it whispers drowsily. In the hotel dining room, someone starts playing the piano. The evening is turning into night, and it's going to be a gorgeous one, for someone. The moon is a thin white wafer in the sky. The wrap-around veranda provides a shadowed place for me to stand and just breathe. I lean against a chair, trembling.

Oh, Sim. What a horrible thing to do to poor, stupid Topher.

At least now I know what happened at the party. I wonder whether, if I had gone, I would have been the friend who was conveniently on hand when things went wrong. I can't believe Topher was so gullible. . . . I run my fingers through my hair and sigh. Topher isn't the only one.

"I owe you one, Laine." I shake my head. There's no point in denying that Sim used me too. He needed more than my physics notes. He needed me to be his audience, to admire him and keep on coming back when he blew me off. He was like the worst restaurant critic, tasting dish after dish after dish of the house's best and saying there was something wrong with each of them.

Why is this hitting me so hard? Because I thought I was someone special? That I was the only one he used?

"You're one sick chick," I mutter to myself, pinching the bridge of my nose.

Topher's probably tired of waiting for me. I steel myself to endure the half-hour ride back out to the cabin. He probably won't even speak to me, but that doesn't matter. I wonder if I can talk Mom into letting us go home early. All I want is for this vacation to end.

A glance around the well-lit lobby and panic hits my stomach. I step into the entrance of the dining room, and waves of humiliation break over me. Not only has this been the worst dinner ever, it looks like Topher has ditched me. I hurry back to the porch, down the stairs, and into the parking lot. The van isn't there.

I can feel my chin quivering. I must look like I'm about six and lost, and I hate myself for it, for being lost, for being so stupid as to get left behind, and for getting weepy about it. What do I do now? There's no cell service. I don't know the number to the cabin. I wasn't thinking I'd ever have to know it. I feel stupid and unprepared. Even if I could find a bus or a taxi, who knows where the cabin is?

There's a breeze kicking up, and the headlights of occasional cars are the biggest illumination out here between the yellowy streetlights, high above the road. I watch the road for a few minutes before I realize there's nothing else to do. I start walking.

There are no stars out yet, so there is nothing to wish on. I trip on the toe of my shoe and stumble. A car comes up behind me, windows down. Music jangles on the quiet night air, and someone yells, "Have a nice trip! See you next fall!" followed by hoots and laughter.

If I could ball myself up and become invisible, I would.

Every time headlights come around the corner, I cringe. A blocky little minivan does a U-turn behind me, and I hear my name.

"Elaine!"

I wait for another car to pass, then cross the road quickly. Topher glares at me as he pushes open the door. "What the hell are you doing?! I've been looking for you for fifteen minutes!"

"Me? I didn't go anywhere until I saw you'd left!"

"I 'left'? I didn't leave! I even made some girl look for you in the bathroom." Topher is livid. "Jeez, Elaine."

"I just stood on the porch. I didn't see you. . . ." My voice trails away.

Topher blows out a sigh. "Whatever. Get in the car." He doesn't say anything else to me all the way back, and the distance to the cabin seems longer than I remember.

This is the worst, worst, *worst* time I have had with anyone in my whole life. I am sick, but I can't throw up. There is no way to rid me of myself, which is all that's making me ill. I can't believe how badly this has gone. I can't believe the mess I've made.

When we reach the cabin, there are white lights twinkling along the deck. Cars are lined up along the street. The Haineses are throwing a party, I remember, and my stomach knots. How am I supposed to walk into the hallway and through the living room to be examined by a whole host of strangers before I can reach the safety of my room? I think I might be sick for real.

Topher puts the car in park and snatches out the keys. It takes him a moment to realize that I'm not moving. He leans back impatiently, hand on the wheel.

"Are you just going to sit there?"

"No."

"Well, get out, then." Topher's voice is mean.

I know I should thank him for dinner, but there's really no good spin to put on this night. I feel like my head is trapped in a vise. "Topher, look—"

Topher slams the door. "Save it, Elaine."

I jerk open my door and stand to face him. "You're not being fair! Topher, I didn't know what happened to you, okay? I didn't know! Do you think I'd be sitting here defending that or, or, applauding because you got arrested?"

"I don't know what you'd do." Topher stops, keys clenched in his fist. "I really have no idea."

"Well, I wouldn't. I'm sorry it happened, Topher."

"'It' happened? What's 'it'? The probation? The random drug tests? The drug possession that's now on my record? Do you know I might have to wait a year now to apply for college? That I might have lost all my student loans? Which 'it' are you sorry happened, Elaine?"

I am shaking. Topher leans close, still spitting venom.

"Nothing's ever going to be the same for me, Elaine, nothing. So, don't you stand there and say your little 'sorrys' to me."

"I didn't know." My voice is barely above a whisper. "He didn't invite me to the party. . . ." I look up. "Topher, didn't you tell somebody? Didn't you tell your parents it was him?"

Topher rolls his eyes. "Laine, who are they gonna believe, me or some lawyer's kid? The cops weren't listening to anybody that night. I didn't tell anybody anything. It was my fault for believing he'd have my back. Keller's never had anybody's back but his own."

Topher blows out a sigh. "Anyway." He turns back toward the house, then looks back at me, shaking his head as if to clear it. "It's not . . . I didn't mean to blow up at you anyway. It's just . . . I can't stand that you would be with somebody like him."

"I . . . wasn't. He just . . . He's changed a lot since junior high."

"I have too, Elaine." Topher's voice is raw. "Do you think you'll ever see that?"

"I—I don't . . . Topher, I . . ."

The screen door slaps, and I jump. Someone comes out of the house, and light shows in the open doorway.

"Oh, hey! You're back!"

I know what this must look like—Topher and me standing in the dark by the car. I look at Topher. Mr. Haines will see I look like I've been crying, and we need to get our stories straight before we go in. Mom's going to want to hear all about how great a time we had, and neither of us looks happy enough to pull that off.

"Hey, Dad. We just got here," Topher says.

"Oh. Well." Mr. Haines glances back over his shoulder and comes down the stairs. "Did you get the steak?"

Topher nods. "Like always."

Mr. Haines crosses the yard, slowly approaching the car. "So, what are you two going to do now? Your mom dug up some slides. . . ."

"Oh, Lord," Topher groans.

Mr. Haines grins. "She's showing the trip to Budapest and Hungary we took two years ago. I'd almost forgotten you had braces, Toph."

Topher's mouth tightens. "Dad."

"Well, you never know. Maybe Laine would like to—"

Laine would not like to do anything but escape, thank you.

"Actually, I was just going up to bed." Is that my voice that sounds so weird?

Mr. Haines is deliberately hearty. He leans on the hood, peering into my face. "You sure you want to do that? Do you play pool? How about we get out some old video games or pull out another movie from the archives?"

I know he sees that I've been crying. Why won't he leave me alone? "I think I'll just go upstairs."

"You sure? Lainey, you're our guest. We'd love to have your company." There's something in Mr. Haines's voice.

"Dad." Topher sounds resigned. "I'll play pool with you."

Mr. Haines looks up hopefully at me. "Lainey? You sure you don't want our company?"

Don't want his company? What can I say? "I . . . I'll go change."

"Great! When you come down, we might talk Ana

into making some divinity," Mr. Haines calls over his shoulder, walking away. "It's good stuff."

My legs are trembling as I walk up the stairs. I'm not up to being good company. I don't want to try. And Mr. Haines's transformation from a quiet, geeky engineer to a man bent on turning me into a happy camper exhausts me.

I am glad to close the door on the sounds of the party, but Ana knocks on my door a few minutes later and calls out that she'll meet me in the kitchen. When I open the door, I hear Mr. Haines tell the group in the living room that Ana's divinity is not to be missed. When I step into the hallway, Topher is there.

"Elaine." His voice is hushed. "About my parents. My dad . . . he thinks I went to Sim's party and all because he and Mom didn't pay enough attention to me. So, the pool thing . . . You don't have to play if you don't want to. Dad's just been . . . making sure we spend time and stuff." He shrugs.

"Oh, Topher." I take a shaky breath. "I'm sorry." I swallow. "I'll play. I at least owe you a game of pool for ruining your evening, don't I?"

Topher raises his chin, mouth taut, slate eyes unsmiling. "You don't owe me *anything*."

I half smile. "Yeah, I know. And that's why it'll be fun beating you."

A faint smile softens Topher's face. He shakes his head. "We'll see."

As it turns out, the evening is not so bad. Playing with an engineer and his son, I lose—badly—at pool. Ana makes her noxiously sweet divinity, which people apparently love, even though it's the consistency of hardening glue. Mr. Haines heats up the last few pieces of last night's dessert, the peach apple crisp, and insists that everyone have a microscopic taste. I get lots of polite adult praise, but I know no one could have had a bite big enough to appreciate it. On a positive note, one guy, Michael Something-or-other, says he'd like to taste something else I make sometime. He works for a newspaper in the Bay Area. Maybe he'll come up and do a nice write-up for Mom.

I throw myself into faking a good time. By evening's end, Topher's happier, Mom is beaming, and the Haineses think I'm "such a nice girl."

Mission accomplished, right?

BASIC BREAKFAST CRÊPES

MAKES ABOUT 10 SERVINGS

* * FOR CRÊPES * *

2 C. ALL-PURPOSE FLOUR

PINCH OF SALT

~~1/3 C. GRANULATED SUGAR~~ (NOT REALLY NECESSARY?

MAKES THEM BROWN BETTER... OPTIONAL)

3 EGGS

1 C. MILK

2 TSP. VANILLA EXTRACT

1 TBSP. BUTTER (OKAY USING 2 TSP.)

IN A BOWL, COMBINE FLOUR, SALT, AND SUGAR. MIX IN EGGS AND STIR UNTIL LUMPS DISSOLVE. MIX IN MILK, THEN VANILLA EXTRACT AND MELTED BUTTER.

HEAT NON-STICK SAUTÉ PAN, THEN SPRAY WITH VEGETABLE PAN SPRAY. PLACE 4 TBSP. BATTER IN PAN, THEN COOK OVER LOW FLAME UNTIL CRÊPE APPEARS DRY.

REMOVE CRÊPE FROM PAN AND ALLOW TO COOL BEFORE HANDLING. REPEAT TO MAKE 10.

* * SAINT JULIA SAYS FRENCH CHEFS LET THE CRÊPE BATTER
SIT FOR AT LEAST AN HOUR BEFORE USING IT.

* * ROTATE THE PAN A LITTLE IF YOU'RE COOKING ON A
WEIRD STOVE OR AN ELECTRIC WITH UNEVEN HEAT!!!
DON'T MESS WITH THE CRÊPE UNTIL IT'S DRY, OR IT'LL
COME APART. (IT MAY COME APART ANYWAY.)

* * THE FIRST CRÊPE IS FOR THE DOG. FIRST CRÊPES NEVER
TURN OUT RIGHT.

* * FOR FILLING * *

6 TBSP. JUICE-SWEETENED BERRY JAM (LOGANBERRY IS REALLY
GOOD!)
6 TBSP. WATER
3/4 C. FRESH BERRIES (FROZEN WORKS TOO. IF YOU USE
FROZEN, SKIP THE WATER)

MIX
~~ADD~~ JAM AND WATER AND BERRIES ~~ADD~~ AND COOK OVER A LOW FLAME
UNTIL JAM AND WATER COMBINE AND THICKEN AND BERRY
JUICE COOKS DOWN A LITTLE. (DON'T USE MICROWAVE.) THIS
TAKES ABOUT 10 MINUTES OR SO. IT'S BASICALLY BERRY
SYRUP WITH CHUNKS. IF YOU USE FROZEN BERRIES
WITH LITTLE SEEDS, YOU MIGHT WANT TO STRAIN IT — ?

PLOP ABOUT 2 TBSP. OF FILLING INTO EVERY CRÊPE, THEN
FOLD IN HALF.

* * YOU CAN ADD RICOTTA, BUT IF YOU'RE OUT, YOU
CAN EAT IT WITH COTTAGE CHEESE. OR PLAIN.

16

Just a few days ago, I would have called you crazy for saying I'd miss Christopher Haines for *any* reason, but I'm not looking forward to a three-hour ride home from Yosemite with just Mom. Though the last day or two of vacation was at least a nominal cease-fire, Mom still hasn't given up the idea that she should organize my life as well as she organizes the spices in the cabinet at home. She's been bugging me about finding an internship again, asking what plans Topher has for his life, and even asking me if I ever heard Simeon talk about what he wanted to do in life, as if she can subtly discover his whereabouts.

In the car, I brace for another round of Vivianne Seifert's Twenty Questions, but Mom surprises me this time by not asking me anything. She puts on the stereo and we listen to, ridiculously, a relaxation CD, bubbling brooks interspersed with wafting flutes. By the time we're out of Yosemite Valley, it's like water torture. I need a bathroom, and I'm fighting back giggles.

"Mom. Are you tense? 'Cause all this water makes me have to pee."

Mom's mouth twitches. "Sorry. I thought it would help."

I find myself smiling. "Thanks. . . . But I don't need any 'help.' I'm fine."

Mom flicks a glance at me sideways. "Are you?"

"Not really, but who is?" I shrug. "It's just life, Mom."

"Can we talk about it?" my mother asks gently. And then her phone rings.

"Answer it."

Mom gives me an incredulous look. "Not on your life! Lainey, you are far more important to me than any-one on the other end of that line. Believe me, it can wait."

"But . . ." I don't really have anything to say. "It's nothing, Mom. Answer the phone."

For a moment, Mom's shoulders slump, but then she straightens. "I'm going to keep asking, Lainey," she says. "I'm asking because I love you."

"I know, Mom," I say. "Answer the phone."

Mom sighs and punches the button to activate her headset.

I'm relieved. I don't want to talk to Mom anymore

about Simeon. She's going to say he wasn't a good influence for me or something like that, that I'm a "great girl" and I'll find someone who meets my high standards, blah blah. The thing is, his leaving still hurts, and what Topher told me hurts worse. I'm just not ready for the "lemons make lemonade" pep talk yet.

Mom stays on the phone all the way home. For the first time, I realize how much she's put off to spend time with me. There are restaurant people and wedding coordinators and others who have left messages for her already today. There's a food magazine that wants a shot of a certain dish and needs to schedule people. In between calls Mom's been making voice memos to herself about things to do later. Once, I clear my throat, and she stops talking to glance at me.

"Did you want to say something?"

"Umm . . . no."

A sigh. "Laine? Is there a specific reason you don't want to talk to me?"

My stomach twists. "You want to fix everything. . . . Plus, you don't like him."

"I didn't know we were talking about 'him.'" She says it mildly, but I still react.

"We're not. But . . . I don't want you to say 'I told you so.'"

A pause. "When have I ever said that I don't like Simeon?"

"Well, you don't. You acted like I was wasting my time by being friends with him."

Mom sighs and changes lanes. "Remember when I told you that a great girl like you would find all kinds of people to appreciate her someday? I meant that. Elaine, it's *never* a waste to be a friend to someone, and I've never objected to you being a friend to Simeon. What I've objected to is you pretzeling yourself around what he wants to the point that you're cutting me off and changing who you are."

"I haven't changed," I say defensively. "I'm the same person I always was."

"So this time last year you were someone who lied to me and withdrew from my bank account without telling me? No. Don't you see? Lainey, you compromised my trust. You put Simeon's wants above your own knowl-edge of what was right. And now"—she grimaces—"you keep wondering why I can't get past it. You know why I can't? Because I don't think you understand yet how serious this was. What else are you willing to do for a friend, Elaine? How much are you willing to give away?"

There's an uncomfortable silence. Mom breaks it.

"I love you, Lainey. You know I do. And I'm sorrier than you know that Simeon is gone and there's no reso-lution for you. I won't say I'm not relieved you're no longer involved with him, but it's not about *him*, Lainey. My concern is all about you."

Was that an "I told you so"? Or did I already know that?

It's the last week for pea shoots. Mom, Pia, and the sous-chef have discussed changing some items on the menu to later-spring dishes, like grilled vegetables, but I still find myself with a sink full of the delicate greens, washing them carefully. I feel like I've been standing elbow deep in water for the last week, but I'm happy to be back in the kitchen.

Mom decided that I don't need to check in with her at the restaurant anymore, but I've been coming in every evening anyway, mostly because being alone in the house gives me too much time to think. I stay up late and sleep in. I watch reruns of *Baking with Julia*, and I flip through my notebooks, Mom's cookbooks, and all my food magazines to find something new to create every day. I even make a time-consuming mu shu, from the thin pancakes to the filling to the sauce. There are still too many hours to fill.

There hasn't been any word from Simeon, and the number I had for him has been disconnected. The gray spy car wasn't here when we got home. It's like he no longer exists. I don't know what to think.

Every night, I walk, taking a roundabout way to La

Salle, and try to get everything out of my system. It's really starting to hit me that I have nothing to do, no one to try to organize but myself. I'm slowly starting to take the idea of an internship seriously. I'll probably need to find a paying internship, since I doubt I'll see Simeon again with my money, and Mom's account isn't open to me anymore. Suddenly the shape of the future looks really, really different, and I don't know how I feel about it. Life—real life—is approaching fast.

I walk with quick, determined steps, and I'm a block past the hospital before I start to slow down. It's a warm night in San Rosado. People are just getting home from work, and there's a banner over the road, between Sophie Lane and Mulberry, advertising the First Street Festival to coincide with the farmers' markets again this season.

There's a crowd in front of Copperfield's, sitting at the open-air tables and chatting. I can smell coffee mingling with the harsher smell of smoke as people unwind with their newspapers and cell phones. A bunch of guys look like they're actually playing some kind of board game while they're drinking their coffee. A huge pair of dice with something like fourteen sides clatters off the table. One of the guys dives into my path to grab it.

"Sorry." I give him a half smile and keep going. He's kind of cute, in a completely mad-scientist, antisocial way, but it makes me depressed that he's outside on a nice evening playing a game with a bunch of geeky guys. Where's the romance in the world?

There's a vendor in front of Soy to the World, selling tie-dyed scarves and dolphin toe rings. I sidestep her warily. All I need is someone trying to talk to me about peace and love. I know my walk is turning into a pity party, but I can't help it. I feel like everything that *could* unravel with my life *has*.

Everywhere I look, there are people wandering out in the balmy evening air, looking happy with their world and completely absorbed in their friends. The library is having a used-book sale, and I stop for a moment to browse. I'm always on the lookout for old cookbooks. I flip through a few, then sigh and keep walking. Even cooking doesn't seem worthwhile.

Tonight the restaurant seems foreign to me. I feel like I'm in the way. Mom and Pia are busy, running around and making special orders. Ming asked if I've found my internship yet, and Gene wanted to hear about my college choices, but things got busy when a huge party came in and everyone had to move tables and recheck the menu to accommodate food allergies. One of the diners is allergic to *lettuce*. Seriously.

By the time the rush is over, I've paced Mom's office like a caged panther, gone down to the kitchen twice to watch everyone running around, and refused a plate when Pia offered me one, and now I'm standing at the back door, watching the little slice of sky visible from the alley where the busboys take their smoke breaks. The clouds have rolled in. It's threatening to rain or at least get unpleasantly foggy and make my hair frizz up all over my head.

My mother appears next to me and puts her hand on my shoulder. The two of us stand quietly, watching the storm come.

I keep hearing what Mom said to me, about how much I'm willing to give away to keep a friend. Was I willing to trade *her*? Was she just being overdramatic? I'd like to think so, but I remember how I felt when I thought Simeon needed me. When I start thinking that Mom's got it all wrong, I remember how good it felt, how much it filled me, and then I wonder . . . is she right?

The first week back to school always sucks, but this first week of the last grading period is really "craptacular," as Cheryl says. For one thing, it's the beginning of senior countdown, and all I see everywhere is signs about the prom, the Last Dance, which is Redgrove's cheap and casual all-school party for those who can't afford the prom, and all final projects, final tests, and final everythings. The eight weeks ahead loom like an overstuffed burrito; niceties like time to sleep, put on makeup, or eat seem to have fallen messily by the wayside. Every night that I'm not at the restaurant, I'm at a tutoring session for either physics or trigonometry.

The good news is that I got into the California Culinary Academy in San Francisco, starting in the summer if I want it or fall if I don't, and I got in at Mills College with an "undeclared" major, and I'm wait-listed for UC Berkeley. The bad news is, our teachers keep saying that acceptance letters are no guarantee if our grades tank these last few weeks, so I know I'd better keep on top of things. When I find out that Cheryl is a tutor for English lit, I wonder briefly what it would take to bribe her into writing my last paper for me. Cheryl just laughs when I ask her.

Vocal Jazz has added even more urgency to life with an impending performance. Our upcoming spring show means that zero period turns into boot camp each morning and Ms. Dunston puts us through our paces.

The second week after break, I get a letter from the *Just Tomatoes* contest I entered. It is polite, a "thank you for taking the time to enter our contest, your entry was very creative" type of form letter, but a rejection is a rejection no matter how nicely they put it. This is kind of the last straw. I am so depressed I don't even go to the gym, even though I know the corn bread I baked from scratch for last night and the bag of kettle corn I bought at the cafeteria snack shop on Friday have made themselves at home in my body somewhere. What makes it worse is that the kettle corn didn't even taste all that good.

As is the tradition at Redgrove, the seniors "surprise" Ms. Dunston at our last Vocal Jazz rehearsal before the show. One of the tenors, who went to Hawaii with his family for break, brings a two-pound box of chocolate-covered macadamia nuts. Ms. Dunston opens the box at the end of class, and I am feeling so crappy I eat three pieces. There are 204 calories in an *ounce* of plain macadamia nuts. I don't even want to know how many calories there are if you add chocolate. I only hope I can fit into my Jazz uniform one last time.

Backstage at the spring show Friday night has the feel of the kitchen at La Salle. Between numbers, the jazz band plays swing music, and we can hear the audience applauding soloists, dancers, and instrumentalists. Every few minutes some minor drama breaks out, and hysterical giggling is shushed or someone starts sniffling or rushes off to the bathroom. The theater girls, in copper satin dresses, are clustered in front of mirrors, pinning fake white roses in their hair for the final piece. The Vocal Jazz group, the girls in hideous teal dresses and the guys in matching vests, is just getting ready for its cue. We're holding no music, no props, nothing. Our final performance is like a prix fixe menu, a smorgasbord of the year's performances, and only Ms. Dunston, chic in a little black dress with diamond pins in her hair, knows what our encore will be. This performance counts for a third of our grade.

"Hey, Laine." Topher is standing next to me, looking cautious. "Good luck tonight."

I smile over at him. The teal makes his dark gray eyes stand out. "You too. I just hope we don't have to sing 'Java Jive' for the encore."

Topher opens his mouth to say something else, but Ms. Dunston hisses, "Places!" and all chattering ends as we quickly shift into position. I catch Topher's smile and return his quick thumbs-up. This is it—our last song.

Applause washes over us as we stride onstage. Of course, Mom took an hour or so off from La Salle, and I look out into the audience, blinded by the footlights and flashes from hundreds of cameras, hoping to see her. As my eyes wander over the darkened auditorium, I glimpse someone standing by the side entrance, leaning against the wall with his arms crossed. My brain identifies Simeon Keller long before my eyes do. I suck in a huge breath.

The basses start the first notes to Ellington's "It Don't Mean a Thing," and I'm caught off guard. I glance at Ms. Dunston, and she's pointing at the altos. We come in, our "doo-wop, doo-wop, doo-wop" synchronized perfectly with the tenors, just like we've practiced. I snap my fingers with the rest of my section on cue, but my stomach is roiling. What's he doing here? Was that really him?

It's a busy song, full of quick changes and tandem

movements, and I can't afford to get lost. Finally, we reach our big finish, but when I glance that way again, nobody's there. It's crazy. He wouldn't come back now, I know, and certainly not back to a school show. But still, there's a deep disappointment that drags at me throughout our performance. Even the encore, "A Quiet Place"—my all-time favorite song—does nothing for my mood. I skip the after-show reception and opt to leave with Mom.

"You looked like you were having fun up there tonight," my mother says. She turns down the street from the school and merges into the busy traffic. "If the food business doesn't work out for you, maybe you can hire yourself out in Las Vegas."

"Oh, *nice.*" I mock-scowl. "Like I haven't had enough with the sequins and I need *feathers.*" I touch my fingertips to the rose Ms. Dunston got all of her seniors. I feel a little melancholy. Already the edges of the petals are curling.

"Sure you don't want to wear this in the kitchen? All the line chefs will want to see it."

I laugh and look down at my finery. "Yeah. I can hear them now. No, I'll just change and be over in about an hour."

"Why don't you drop me at La Salle and drive back? It's still a little drizzly for walking."

"Mom, I *need* to walk after standing still in these stupid

shoes all night. Don't worry about it, okay? A little rain won't melt me."

My mother makes a noncommittal noise and smiles. Since we've been back, I've sensed that she's been trying to keep her distance, trying not to order and organize me quite so much. It's still a struggle for her, but she's trying. In return, I'm trying not to mind so much when she does look at me and sees what I could be instead of what I am. Maybe it's part of being a mother, maybe it's a management skill she's picked up from La Salle, but I am learning to live with it and with her.

At home, I slip out of the hated teal dress one last time and wonder gleefully which unlucky underclassman will inherit it from me. Pulling the pins out of my hair, I wind it into a simple bun on the nape of my neck, relieved to be looking more like myself. The front door closes, and I grab my sweatshirt and jog down the stairs, smothering my irritation.

"Mom, I said you didn't have to wait. . . ." My voice trails off as I realize the room is empty. "Mom?"

I come down the last few stairs, frowning. As I reach the door, I glance at the coffee table. I see my name on an envelope in a familiar scrawl, and it hits me. It was not my imagination.

I snatch open the door.

"Simeon!"

SHREDDED VEGETABLE MU-SHU STYLE ROLLUPS

* * SAUCE * *

(OR USE STORE BOUGHT HOISIN, BUT THIS IS QUICK AND GOOD.)

1/4 C. SOY SAUCE

2 TBSP. DRY COOKING SHERRY

1 TBSP. SUGAR OR SUGAR SUBSTITUTE

1 TBSP. SESAME OIL

BLACK PEPPER, FRESHLY GROUND

* * FILLING * *

2 TBSP. GINGER, PEELED AND MINCED

(SMASH ON CUTTING BOARD WITH BROAD KNIFE, THEN MINCE)

3 1/2 OZ. MUSHROOMS, FRESH

(SHIITAKE IS GOOD, BUT WHATEVER YOU CAN FIND WILL WORK)

1 lb. CABBAGE

15 TINY CARROTS, PREPACKAGED, WASHED, AND PEELED

8 MEDIUM SCALLIONS, BOTTOMS ONLY, WASHED AND JULIENNED

1 TBSP. OIL, VEGETABLE

STORE-BOUGHT WHEAT FLOUR ASIAN PANCAKES OR, IF YOU'RE
   DESPERATE, USE THIN BURRITO SHELLS.

MAKE SAUCE FIRST. IN A MEASURING CUP, MIX THE
SOY SAUCE, SHERRY, SUGAR, SESAME OIL, AND SOME PEPPER.

CUT STEMS FROM MUSHROOMS, AND WIPE THEM CLEAN. SLICE
THINLY. TO SAVE TIME, USE FOOD PROCESSOR TO SHRED THE
CABBAGE AND CARROTS, BUT CUT UP THE CABBAGE FIRST,
IN CHUNKS THAT WILL FIT.

WHEN ALL THE INGREDIENTS ARE PREPPED AND YOU'RE READY,
HEAT THE VEGETABLE OIL OVER MEDIUM-HIGH HEAT IN A
LARGE POT. ADD THE GINGER, MUSHROOMS, CABBAGE, AND
CARROTS WHEN OIL IS HOT. STIR-FRY BRIEFLY, THEN ADD
SCALLIONS AND SOY-SHERRY SAUCE. LOWER THE HEAT TO
MEDIUM AND CONTINUE TO STIR. IT SHOULD TAKE ONLY
ANOTHER 2 MINUTES BEFORE VEGETABLES ARE TENDER.
DO NOT STOP STIRRING. IT'S STIR-FRY.

HEAT YOUR ASIAN PANCAKES OR THE ~~TORTILLAS~~ BURRITOS IN THE
MICROWAVE ON A DINNER PLATE BETWEEN DAMP PAPER TOWELS
FOR 45 SECONDS. SPREAD A THIN LAYER OF HOISIN SAUCE,
TOP WITH A TABLESPOON OF ~~MUSHU~~ MU SHU, AND ROLL UP.
IT'S MESSY BUT WORTH IT.

✳ ✳ KEEP THE ASIAN PANCAKES COVERED WITH THE
DAMP PAPER TOWEL OR THEY'LL DRY OUT AND
BE USELESS.

✳ ✳ DON'T OVERHEAT ~~TORTILLAS~~ BURRITOS IF YOU ~~CAN~~ USE THEM
— THEY GET CRISPY.

17

He hasn't changed much—maybe a bit thinner, his dyed-black hair a bit longer and darker, but mostly he's just the same. He bounds up the stairs, wraps his arms around me, and squeezes until I squeak.

"How ya been, Laine?"

"Simeon—were you just going to leave?" I sputter, pushing back from his chest. "You jerk! Where have you been? What happened? Why didn't you text me?"

Sim holds up a hand. "Whoa, whoa. It's great to be back, *Mom*," he teases, squeezing me again and grinning. "You don't know how much I've missed having someone ask me when I'm coming home and stuff."

"All right, fine," I say, hugging him again. "Simeon, it's so good to see you."

"It's good to see you too." He grins. "You were great at the spring show."

"Thanks! I thought I saw you, and then you were gone. . . . Sim, your parents—did you know they hired an investigator? Have you seen them?"

Sim shrugs good-naturedly, tucking a piece of hair behind my ear. "Yeah, I heard. I've already been by to see them and that's settled. I'm eighteen. There was a lot of drama, but we're done."

"Oh . . ." I pause, at a loss. "Well. So, what's been going on? Where have you been?"

Sim grins. "Around. I took a little detour, but eventually I got where I was going."

I feel a little annoyed. "And where was that? I got worried when you didn't at least text me to say you got to Washington okay, and then I tried the youth hostel and—"

Sim shrugs again. "Oh—yeah. I hooked up with a couple of guys from the University of Washington first thing and crashed out in their dorm for a couple of days. And then I found a roommate, picked up a gig at a coffee shop, and things started jumpin'." Sim's smile is smug, and that smugness sizzles on my nerves like water on a hot pan.

"Well, you could have told me where you were. I thought something . . . happened."

"Something did happen, Laine! I found a couple of guys who have this amazing apartment right near University Village, and they sublet it to a guy who isn't working out . . . so if I play my cards right, I'm in. I've got a job, and things are looking good for once. Everything is coming together."

"Well. Great," I say, my voice falsely cheerful. "Glad it all worked out for you. I wish I'd known you were coming. Mom would have loved to see you. In fact, I was just—"

Sim wrinkles his nose. "Oh no, I'm only here to pick up a couple of things from some friends," he says carefully. "I don't have time to see people. But I'm glad you caught me. I would have hated to miss you!" He squeezes me again, but this time I am not overwhelmed just by having him here. I step back in the circle of his arms and look at him seriously.

"Sim? Have you seen . . . Topher Haines?"

Simeon stills. "Um, no. Should I?"

I look up into his strange yellow-amber eyes. "Topher told me something," I begin slowly. "About your party."

Simeon shakes his head. "Yeah, that kind of sucked, huh? We were all so busted, and then Topher gets caught holding the bag. That was pathetic, wasn't it? He wasn't even loaded."

"You didn't give it to him, Sim?"

Simeon shrugs. "Ah, I don't remember. That wasn't a great night, Laine. So, how is 'Chris Topher'? Everything worked out in the end, huh?"

"He really got screwed, Sim. It wasn't right."

"Yeah." Simeon shrugs easily. "That happens. Could've happened to me too."

Is that it? I wait for him to say something, anything, to dispute what Topher said. Instead, he glances down at me and discards the topic like an empty paper cup.

"So, five weeks till graduation, huh? You coming out to Seattle this summer, Laine?"

"No." The word pops out unexpectedly, surprising me with its force. "No," I say again, more sure now. "I'm going to D.C., to the Smithsonian. I'm doing an internship somewhere. And then there's culinary school, probably in the spring, when I've worked a little. I'm going to be busy this summer. I won't have time."

"Really?" Sim's forehead wrinkles in surprise. "That's hard-core."

I smile faintly, feeling the knowledge tremble, newborn inside me. "Not really. It's just . . . I know what I want to do."

Sim nods slowly, looking at me steadily. "You do." It's a statement. "That's cool."

We kind of stand and look at each other, and then Simeon brushes his fingers over my cheek. "I've thought about you a lot, Laine," he says softly.

"Not enough to call, though, huh?" I smile back, almost sad that I know it's so true.

Sim laughs shortly. "Man, Laine, you're brutal. Okay, so I screwed up." His finger traces my lower lip. "I'll make it up to you, okay? Come see me this summer?"

Now he asks, when all I have ever wanted was for him to ask me to see him. All I have ever wanted was for him to want me with him, to need me to be around, to take notice of what I do. But . . . now it's not what I want anymore. I'm not a girl who's meant to be a side dish. I won't stand around and wait for some boy while he chooses me. I can choose me too.

"I've got things to do, so I doubt it," I say easily. No promises, no expectations. "Take care of yourself. Don't do anything too stupid."

"You too, Laine." Sim's expression is hard to read as he bends and kisses me, tentatively, gently, as if asking a question. I kiss him softly, exploring his mouth, feeling chills as his hands trace patterns up my back. When we take a breath, I step back, feeling . . . thoughtful.

Rachel Sconza was right. Simeon Keller is a darned good kisser. But that's not good enough, not for me. I don't need whatever it is he's finally offering me. Not anymore. It's too little, and it's too late. I don't know exactly when it happened, but whatever I found attractive in the gorgeous boy with his arms around me isn't there anymore. It's like I don't know who he is.

Sim brushes his lips over my forehead, then drops his

arms, his eyes intent on mine. "Take care. I'll be in touch." His hand slips down my arm, holds my fingers, finally lets go.

I stand in the doorway until he's gone, feeling like I'm watching a stranger walk away.

If the perfect state could be achieved by shopping, I would have reached a state of Zen-like Nirvana by spending a couple of afternoons with Dea. As it is, I come away with two pairs of flip-flops and some studded leather boots that were on clearance, which is a pretty good start. I'm still feeling stress from finals and am a little unsettled from Sim's visit, but shopping with my grandmother makes the world brighter.

I told Mom that Sim had dropped by and surprised us both by bursting into tears as I told her about his party and what Topher had told me at Yosemite. Once she got that Simeon hadn't done anything to me, she set herself to organizing my life so I could be happy again—and organizing Topher's life too, calling Ana and commiserating with her on the telephone. Poor Topher. I'm sure he thought he had enough trouble.

MaDea has been coming by a couple of weekends a month just to "spend some time," as she says. She cooks with me, giving me her secret recipe for perfect lemon cake, biscuits, peas, and rice. She also takes me shoe-shopping, which is her cure for all the ills in the world.

"If you won't eat any potato chips, at least try on those turquoise sandals," she urges me. "Those rhinestones ought to cheer you up."

Mom's started coming home later and later as she eases up enough to give herself a break from trying to be everywhere I am. One Friday when she's been in and out of the house all afternoon, she says she's going to drop by the restaurant and then come and check back with me.

"You've been so quiet lately. When I get back, we'll have some coffee," Mom says, which translates: *Summer is coming; let's talk some more about how I can organize you.*

The thought of a capital *T* talk makes me antsy. I'm not in the mood for another conversation with Mom on "how things are going." We haven't really had time lately to say anything deep or serious, and I've just been concentrating on getting up in the morning and wading through the incoming tide of papers, tests, and final projects. I'm busy. What does she mean, I've been quiet? What does she want from me? Piqued, I pull on my Redgrove cap, grab my sweatshirt, and hit the door.

For a planned escape, the library seems a pretty tame destination, but I can't figure out anywhere else to go. The weather has turned odd again, with a heavy, muggy feel in the air even though it's stopped raining. I'm window-shopping, carrying my books, when I hear the squeal of brakes.

"LAINEY!"

Oh no.

I jump, twist away from the window in panic. Mom's screaming at me from the street, leaning across the passenger seat and waving out the window. I feel a flash of real fear. Mom's not a screamer, not in public, so something must be terribly wrong. She pulls over as I run to the car, tasting metal in my mouth.

"What's wrong?" I gasp, flinging open the door. I sit down. "Is it Dea?"

Mom makes no move to pull away from the curb. Her eyes are huge. "No! Dea's fine. No—Lainey, I tried to call you, but you left your cell in the house. He called! Michael Semple called!"

I'm bewildered, trying to catch my breath. "Michael Semple?"

Mom grabs my arm and shakes it. "Michael . . . SEMPLE, *Michael Semple,* Ana and Kevin's friend. The one who wanted you to cook something for him!"

"Yeah . . . ?" My heart squeezes apprehensively. Mom looks so excited that I'm worried.

"He wants to come to the restaurant and *film* you. He works with the chef from *Bay Café*—it's one of those public-access series that PBS picks up occasionally. He left a message for you to call him."

Film me? My mouth is hanging open.

"Put on your seat belt!" Mom says urgently. "We'll call him from the restaurant!"

I am rubbing my arms, and Mom is still talking. "I thought he worked for the paper! I knew I'd heard his name somewhere before, but I thought for sure I'd met him doing tastings somewhere for the *Clarion*. I had no idea he had any connection with the local scene here." Mom glances at me. "I would have said something."

Film? *Me?*

There is instant chaos as we walk in. Mom is trying to talk to Pia, while Pia, wearing her chef whites and waving a ladle, is trying to talk to Mom. The servers and the undercooks are all whirling around in their complicated ballet, getting ready for dinner service while eavesdropping.

"Michael Semple!" is interrupted by "James Beard Foundation" and "*Michelin.*" Mom and Pia keep babbling as I run down the stairs to the office. I dial our phone number and check the messages. Sure enough, he'd tried to catch me at home.

"Hello, this is Michael Semple; we met at Yosemite about six weeks back? I was hoping to catch Lainey. . . . I've just gotten back here to the city, and we're doing a series on local home cooks called *The Soul of Food.* I wondered if I could talk you into doing a little cooking for me, maybe talking a little about what you cook and why you enjoy it, and if things work out, we might do a little filming. . . . Lainey, if you would give me a call here at the office . . ."

I spin around in Mom's office chair until I am clammy and dizzy. I clutch my elbows, trying to hold myself together.

Six weeks ago! This all started way back then. . . .

"Lainey?" Mom and Pia burst into the office, and Mom looks at me with bright eyes. "Have you called him back?"

Panic rattles my nerves like frozen peas in a stainless steel pot. "It's after three on a Friday . . . shouldn't I call him Monday?"

"No!" Mom and Pia respond in unison.

Pia is emphatic. "Call him now! Call him now!"

"Are you sure?"

"Do it," Mom instructs me, practically bouncing on her toes. "It's always better to return calls right away."

I bite my lip and dial the number. Please, God, make it the machine . . . please . . . please. . . .

The phone rings and clicks over. I sag with relief. "Mr. Semple? This is Lainey Seifert, returning your call. . . ." I leave him a short voice mail, giving him the number for the restaurant, then hang up, hands shaking. Mom and Pia break into applause.

"That's my girl!" Mom cheers. "Oh, Lainey, I'm so excited for you! This could be big!"

"You have to cook here," Pia says decisively. "We'll put the restaurant on the map."

Mom smacks her hand to her forehead. "Lainey! We have to figure out what to cook!"

I blink. "Uh . . . I don't know! Should I make a dessert? Should I make one of Dea's recipes?"

"Give me the phone." Mom perches on the corner of her desk and dials rapidly. "Momma, it's me. Guess what Lainey's gotten into? Television!"

Television? "Mom, he didn't say—" I begin. Pia interrupts, shoving a La Salle Rouge dinner menu into my hands.

"Take a look. Find something to cook for him."

"Wait, Pia," I object. "I don't want to do something fancy. I can't do something from the dinner menu! Can't I just make something easy?"

"He just wants to see you cook," Mom says, pushing the phone into my hand and taking the menu away. "Don't worry about that now. Talk to your grandmother."

"Lainey, I just can't wait to tell that Amelia Johnston. Her granddaughter won a tennis championship. *My* grand-baby's going to be on TV!"

"He didn't say yes for sure," I warn her. "He said 'if things work out.' It's just public access, so—"

"That's nonsense," my grandmother cuts in. "This is going to work out. Are you wearing those new sandals for the show?"

Trust Dea to go right to the heart of the matter. "I don't know," I gasp. "Right now I'm trying to figure out what to cook!"

"Well, don't let your momma choose for you. You're the cook this time, baby girl. And you make that television guy treat you right, you hear?"

Mom interrupts. "Laine, let me talk to her—" Her second line rings, and she says quickly, "Hang on, Momma, that's the other line. Just a second." She switches lines briskly. "La Salle Rouge, this is Vivianne Seifert. . . . Yes, hello, Mr. Semple, she's right here. Just one moment, please."

Mom's eyes are bright, and Pia claps a hand over her mouth as I take the phone. "It's HIM!" Mom mouths, and I feel like I'm going to faint. I hardly recognize the calm voice that comes out of my mouth.

"Hi, Mr. Semple, this is Lainey Seifert. Thank you for asking . . . I'd love to be on your show."

MA DEA'S LEMON LOAF

(ORIGINAL RECIPE, NOT LOWFAT!)

- 3/4 C. UNSALTED BUTTER, MELTED
- 2 C. GRANULATED SUGAR
- 4 EGGS
- 5 LEMONS, PEELED
- 3 C. WHITE FLOUR
- 1 3/4 TSP. BAKING POWDER
- 1 TSP. BAKING SODA
- 1/4 TSP. SALT
- 1-1/4 C. BUTTERMILK

PREHEAT THE OVEN TO 325°F. IN A MEDIUM-SIZED BOWL, CREAM TOGETHER BUTTER AND SUGAR UNTIL SMOOTH. ADD EGGS ONE AT A TIME WHILE MIXING WITH A HAND MIXER. SET MIXTURE ASIDE.

PROCESS LEMON PEELS IN FOOD PROCESSOR UNTIL THE PIECES ARE SMALLER THAN GRAINS OF RICE - THEY SHOULD ALMOST SEEM LIKE A COARSE FLOUR. ADD REMAINING DRY INGREDIENTS TO THE PEELS

IN A LARGER BOWL, COMBINE $1/3$ OF THE DRY MIXTURE
INTO THE CREAMED, THEN MIX IN $1/2$ OF THE BUTTERMILK,
THEN $1/3$ OF THE DRY MIXTURE AGAIN, THEN THE
REMAINING BUTTERMILK FOLLOWED BY THE REMAINING
DRY MIXTURE.

POUR INTO 2 GREASED $9'' \times 5''$ LOAF PANS.
BAKE FOR 50 to 55 MINUTES.

ALLOW TO COOL IN THE PANS BEFORE REMOVING TO
A PLATTER, NOT TO A COOLING RACK.

JUICE SOME OF THE LEMONS AND MIX JUICE WITH SOME
SUGAR. GLAZE COOLED, SLICED CAKES WITH THIS
MIXTURE TO TASTE.

* * THIS IS A SUSPENSION CAKE. SAINT JULIA SAYS
THAT FAILURE TO FOLLOW THE STEPS WILL RESULT
IN UTTER DISASTER! ALL THE INGREDIENTS MIXED OUT
OF ORDER WILL RESULT IN SOMETHING FAR FROM EDIBLE!
IT IS IMPORTANT THAT EACH GRAIN OF SUGAR BE COATED
IN BUTTER AND THEN EGG AND THAT EACH GRANULE
OF LEMON IS COATED WITH FLOUR. IN THIS MANNER,
THE PARTICLES ARE SUSPENDED. OVER-MIXING
WILL DESTROY THE SUSPENSION, AS WILL TRYING
TO RUSH THE THING TOGETHER.
FOLLOW. THE. DIRECTIONS.

Epilogue

There are cameras and video equipment surrounding Mom's test kitchen area at the restaurant. Even though I'm not standing right there, the combined heat from the lights and all the extra people milling around makes the room temperature rise at least fifteen degrees. My armpits are prickly with sweat.

I can't believe how fast everything came together. One minute I'm talking to Mr. Semple, and a week later I'm in the kitchen at La Salle, getting ready to film a segment for *The Soul of Food*.

Mr. Semple is a superb human being. He knew Julia Child! He also knows Alice Waters (which makes him ultra-cool), Jacques Pépin, Kylie Kwong, and the African American pastry chef Beth Setrakian. His assistant, Mr. Dolinsky, has interviewed *hundreds* of five-star chefs. I can't believe that they want to talk to me—just me, plain

Elaine Seifert, from San Rosado. *The Soul of Food* is just a local-access piece for a few TV stations in the area, but Mom says you never can tell where the little roads might lead you. That's what she keeps calling this—"a little road." I feel like I'm in the middle of a superhighway.

I'm watching the action in a computer monitor set back a ways behind the camera. This is where Mr. Semple will stand when the film starts rolling. At the edge of the shot, I can see Mom, looking a little anxious, and MaDea, who is in one of her fanciest tracksuits and is waving to me, newly manicured nails catching the bright light. Pia is dwarfed by Cheryl standing next to her. The camera pans, and I see Topher, who looks up and crosses his eyes for the cameraman. I shake my head and smile.

When I found out I could have a few people observe the shoot, I asked Cheryl after physics if she'd be interested. I've been whipping up a new recipe almost every day, trying to figure out what to cook. Cheryl got the idea that Soy to the World, where she works, could be more than a coffee shop, and get this—she talked her manager, Persephone, into tasting the spelt-flour, lemon poppy-seed bars I made one day. Persephone suggested I make her up a whole tasting tray, and then she said she'd like to take her pick and make a weekly order. Mom just about died of pride over that. I'm pretty shocked too. My first baking job!

Mom tries to tone it down, but she's really, really excited that I'm hanging out with Cheryl—combat boots, brow ring, and all. She's started leaving stuff in the fridge for us to eat after school, but Cheryl doesn't come over to hang out too much. When she's not working at Soy, Cheryl tutors—guess who? Topher Haines.

Mom and I have actually gone over to the Haineses' house a couple of times to socialize recently. When I asked Topher if he wanted to come to the shoot, the look on his face made me laugh out loud. I'm amused to admit it, but the guy's starting to grow on me.

The segment consultant turns to me one more time.

"Okay, Elaine, we're almost ready for you."

I nod. I'm ready, even though the makeup person keeps pressing powder on my sweaty face. I feel stupid, wearing a red T-shirt, Santa hat, and Christmas apron when it's only two weeks till graduation, but I know what Mr. Dolinsky's after. We're working the family angle, he said. He wants me to exude holiday charm, mention the restaurant by name, and talk about my recipe and my holiday memories. I can do that. I still think the hat's a bit much, but we'll see after the first take. Even though Mr. Dolinsky's going to be practically interviewing me, I'm more worried about forgetting what I'm going to say. Panic closes my throat. I gulp, close my eyes, and take a deep breath.

I'm not making anything hard. It's just a gingerbread

house. Mr. Semple said he wanted me to share a cooking memory I have of the holidays, and that's the one I picked.

Mom frowned when she heard my choice. "A gingerbread house? But, Lainey, we only made one once. Don't you want to make MaDea's pecan pie? You can tell how you figured out her secret recipe without her telling you."

"Nope," I told her. "I'll stick with the gingerbread."

Mom doesn't understand, but the memory of the gingerbread house is important. Even though we only made it once, I need to remember it.

I was eleven. Mom made up the dough. I carefully cut out the shapes and baked them, carefully edged the doorways with icing. Sim came over, and we decorated the house with gumdrops and hard candies, chocolate chips and licorice whips. We used chocolate mint candies for shingles and sprinkled sparkly sugar over the wet white icing to make the snow shimmer. When we finally got it all assembled, I was on the verge of tears, I was so excited. It was gorgeous. It was mine. I loved that house. I had such a feeling of pride when it was done.

Mom told me I should enter it in the Culinary Academy's gingerbread house contest.

"Why can't I take it home?" Sim asked me when I wanted to set it in the window. "You and your mom can make another one. I did half the work. . . ."

I remember feeling trapped. Mom didn't say anything. I don't know if she even heard what Sim had asked me. Maybe it wouldn't have made a difference. I just know that somehow I ended up giving him that house even though I didn't want to. I was afraid that if I didn't, he wouldn't be my friend anymore.

He brought it to school the next day, and he and his guy friends tore off the gumdrops, ripped off the roof, and demolished it.

"Lainey gave it to me," I heard him tell one of them as they smacked and gobbled. "She didn't want it."

Breathe, Lainey.

I can feel the air in the kitchen swirling around me. I know what I want, I told Sim, and I do. I want to have friends who really see me and know who I am and what I want. I want to make my dreams come true and have them matter to the people who love me. I want to get in front of the camera and make my gingerbread house and know that it's something I made with my own hands, that it has value. I can do this.

"That's it," I hear Mr. Dolinsky say. "Get in your zone, Lainey. Just pretend you're Julia Child."

"You can do it, Laine," calls Topher. Cheryl gives me a thumbs-up.

"We're ready for you," Mr. Semple says.

Okay, Saint Julia. It's on.

I can hear my tiny television audience applaud. I open my eyes and walk toward the lights.

THE GINGERBREAD HOUSE

1 C. SHORTENING

1 C. SUGAR

1 1/4 C. MOLASSES

1. LARGE EGG

1 TSP. VANILLA EXTRACT

5 1/2 C. UNSIFTED ALL-PURPOSE FLOUR

1 TSP. BAKING POWDER

1/4 TSP. BAKING SODA

2 TSP. FRESHLY GROUND CINNAMON

3 TSP. GROUND GINGER

2 TSP. GROUND CLOVES

1 TSP. NUTMEG

CREAM SHORTENING AND SUGAR. BEAT IN MOLASSES, EGG, AND VANILLA UNTIL SMOOTH. IN ANOTHER BOWL, SIFT DRY INGREDIENTS. GRADUALLY STIR DRY INGREDIENTS INTO MOLASSES MIXTURE. WHEN MIXTURE BECOMES TOO HARD TO STIR WITH A SPOON, WAD UP THE DOUGH WITH YOUR HANDS UNTIL IT'S COMPLETELY MIXED. SEPARATE DOUGH INTO 4 BALLS. WRAP EACH IN PLASTIC WRAP AND CHILL AT LEAST 1 HOUR OR UP TO 2 WEEKS.

** WHEN YOU MAKE YOUR HOUSE, DO IT IN STEPS. BAKE YOUR HOUSE SHAPES ONE DAY, DECORATE THEM THE NEXT, AND BUILD YOUR HOUSE ON ANOTHER DAY. IT'S EASIER THAT WAY, TRUST ME.

SUGAR CEMENT

3 LARGE EGG WHITES AT ROOM TEMPERATURE
  (BE CAREFUL - NO YOLKS OR IT WON'T WORK!)
1/2 TSP. CREAM OF TARTAR
4 3/4 C. POWDERED SUGAR

PLACE EGG WHITES IN BOWL. ADD CREAM OF TARTAR. SIFT SUGAR
DIRECTLY ONTO EGG WHITES. BEAT 4 MINUTES WITH ELECTRIC MIXER
ON HIGH SPEED. THE MIXTURE WILL THICKEN AS YOU BEAT IT
AND WHEN FINISHED SHOULD BE THE CONSISTENCY OF MASHED
POTATOES. PLACE A PIECE OF PLASTIC WRAP DIRECTLY OVER
ICING WHILE USING TO PREVENT AIR FROM DRYING IT.
IF STORING FOR USE AT ANOTHER TIME, STORE ICING IN
AN AIRTIGHT PLASTIC CONTAINER IN THE REFRIGERATOR.
IF ICING BECOMES TOO FIRM, SIMPLY BEAT A LITTLE WATER
INTO IT.

* * USE THE ICING AS "CEMENT" TO PUT THE HOUSE TOGETHER,
  ATTACH DECORATIONS, AND MAKE ICICLES AND DECORATIVE
  TRIM. TWO TO THREE BATCHES ARE NEEDED TO COMPLETE
  1 HOUSE; MAKE EACH BATCH SEPARATELY.

Acknowledgments

Every recipe needs testers. I gratefully acknowledge the writers of WritingYA, especially Sarah "Lareverie" Stevenson, who read every version of this story multiple times with patience and humor and never regarded all of my "treats" as the bribes that they were. To my agent, Steven Chudney, and my editor, Erin Clarke, I also offer thanks—and homemade lemon curd.